ASHLEY JOHNSON

Shifter, Killer and Jelena

A Jelena Cohert Series Novel

F7P
FOREVER SEVEN PRESS
READ, REVIEW, REPEAT

First published by Forever Seven Press 2020

This novel is entirely a work of fiction. The names, characters and incidents portrayed in it are the work of the author's imagination. Any resemblance to actual persons, living or dead, events or localities is entirely coincidental.

Second edition

ISBN: 979-8-9856989-1-6

Editing by Shelley Lopez

This book was professionally typeset on Reedsy.
Find out more at reedsy.com

Contents

The beginning

Lisa stumbled through the woods, her 4-inch heels sinking into the dirt and grass. She had a lot of drinks at the Romano house, so her heels sinking in the dirt were the least of her problems.

Having her clutch in one hand and pepper spray in the other irritated her and made it difficult to balance. She fell to her knees a couple times, tripping so hard she came out of her shoes. She had to stop, put her things down, then put her shoes back on. *Why didn't I ask someone for a ride?* She thought.

As soon as the thought arrived, it fled. She knew why she didn't ask for a ride, she was literally thrown out; she was humiliated.

Excitement flooded her when one of the Romano boys asked her to come over to their house for a party. The Romano's had a lot of siblings, cousins, nieces and nephews. The kids were mostly in junior high and high school. Lisa had some little sisters who were in elementary school, so she knew there were some young Romano's too.

Giovanni Romano was a junior in her high school. He didn't play any sports or anything; but he was great in academics and popular. She thought she'd hit the jackpot when he walked up to her and asked her to come to his house. He said it was a party, that she wouldn't be the only girl. When she got there, she realized there were a lot of Romano boys there, but no girls. It wasn't any type of party she wanted to be at.

She tried to leave, but Giovanni sweet-talked her; he made her feel special. He told her she was early, and all his brothers and cousins live nearby so they had already showed up. Still feeling uncomfortable, she sat down, but *there were more girls coming,* she reassured herself.

They handed her drink after drink while she sat there and waited. A few guys sat next to her, asking her questions. She thought they were trying to get to know her. She needed to have relationships with all the Romano' if she wanted a serious one with Giovanni. She lost track of time after her third cup. She was unsure of what they were giving her. Just that it stung a little going down, had a bitter taste.

The boys packed in around her, making her unable to move. They tossed her clutch across the room and they pinned her arms down. Her heart beat faster in her chest when Giovanni stepped up and grabbed both her legs.

She protested and struggle. "I am ready to go home. Please stop, let me go," she insisted.

She became terrified when Giovanni handed her legs to two other boys and they spread them wide and held on tight. She struggled harder. She screamed until something was stuck in her mouth. Her head was hurting, and she was dizzy.

She became relieved when suddenly everyone let her go.

She heard someone say to Giovanni, "Yo G, I thought you said everyone was at Jordan's house?"

Giovanni's head turned, and she struggled to make out what he was doing. She tried to scoot off the couch, to get to her clutch. She needed to get to her clutch.

She became humiliated when Giovanni picked her up, walked over to the balcony and threw her over the edge. She hit the ground hard, on her shoulder and hip.

Her clutch came flying down after her. She scrambled to it and grabbed her phone and pepper spray from it. She didn't have anyone to call. She couldn't call her parents. What would she tell them? "I went to a party, got drunk, and was almost raped. Then they threw me over a balcony and now I need a ride." Her parents would kill her, she was supposed to be at her best friend's house, anyway.

Lisa fixed her shoes, wiped her face, and began stumbling through the nearby woods.

Her vision was still blurred, her head hurt, and she couldn't walk straight. Lisa sobbed, realizing that she was stuck out here in the woods with no way home.

Just then, she heard a sound. She turned her head quickly and immediately regretted it when her head started pounding furiously. She thought she heard something go past her, like a gust of wind. Lisa groaned, she was really losing it.

She continued to stumble her way through the woods. She stopped again when she heard some type of animal sound, like a mix between a squeal and a growl. "Sober up Lisa, get it together," she told herself. She knew there was no such animal around here.

Suddenly, she felt a sharp pain in her neck and shook violently from side to side. Lisa went to spray whoever was behind her and ended up spraying herself in the face. A piercing scream escaped from her mouth and then everything went black.

Different world

Different World

Jordan walked out on his balcony and sniffed the air. *Smells off,* he thought. Jordan was 6 feet tall and big. He had muscles that rivaled Dwayne "The Rock" Johnson. His family is the lead pack in North America, and he is the Alpha. His hair was short and dark, his eyes a deep brown. Except when the wolf came they sparkled with gold. A brush in the woods ahead caused him to tilt his head slightly to the side. *Who is running on my territory?* he thought.

Jordan sniffed the air again to get a better idea and realized he didn't recognize it. He stuck his head back into the accordion style doors and yelled to his brothers that he was going for a run.

He shut the doors, hoping they would catch the hint and leave their wives to join him. He stripped his clothes off on the balcony and jumped over the railing. By the time he hit the ground, he had transformed into a majestic black wolf with silver fur surrounding his eyes.

He ran over to the pond on his property and admired his reflection in the water. He loved looking at his reflection in his wolf form. As the youngest brother and the only one without a wife and kids, he never thought he would be Alpha of his pack. He never put emphasis on dating and having families because he believed one of his brothers would have the throne next.

Two years ago, his older brother, Jacob, challenged his father for the spot of Alpha. His father had wounded Jacob badly and then when he went in for the kill, something in Jordan snapped. He shifted and went after his father with black and gold in his eyes. His father surrendered after a brutal fight and is now living on the pack property with their mother, having not spoken to Jordan or Jacob since that night, Mesmerized by his reflection, Jordan missed his brothers trotting over to him. Jonathan pounced on him, and the two of them rolled in the water. *What's up, bro?* Jonathan thought telepathically to his brother. Telepathy was a skill shifter had to communicate with each other while they were in their animal form.

Jordan rolled and stood up in the water looking between Jacob and Johnathan. *Someone is on the property,* he told his brothers, *a new scent.* His brothers simultaneously sniffed the air, tilting their head to contemplate the scent. Then the brothers heard a faint scream and bounded off in that direction.

They approached a clearing in their property, about two miles from the Alpha house. They spotted a woman in the middle of a group of trees. Jonathan went to go towards her, but Jordan barked, *No, seems like a trap.*

Jonathan obeyed his Alpha and stayed where he was. Just then a slim, dark haired man, around his brother's heights, each of them coming in at 5'10, came out of the shadows. He had to be a shifter.. Jordan smelled hyena, and hyenas were not to be underestimated.

What are hyenas doing over here? Jacob said to his brothers.

The man responded, seeming to understand their telepathy. "I have some unfinished business in North America," he boasted. The brothers separating to have him covered on all sides. The man rubbed his hands togethe.r "Yes, I'm ready for a fight," he said smugly.

I am Jordan, Jordan Romano, Jordan said. *Alpha of the Romano pack, head of the North American sector.*

The man interrupted. "Titles, titles, titles. I know who you are Jordan, son of John Romano." Jacob silently moved around so that he was coming up on the left side, slipping behind some trees. The man switched his stance, and Jacob stilled.

What business do you have here hyena, who is the woman? Jordan asked. The man stepped aside and picked up the limp woman by her hair. Jordan growled, *Who gave the order to kill that woman,* he bellowed.

"Orders," the man laughed. "Who follows orders anymore? I have killed this one and more like her all around your precious Miami for weeks now. You dogs have been too stupid to notice." The man put his hand on his chin, slightly elevating his head in mock deep thought. "I gather the police should be finding women and making connections by now."

Johnathan took a step forward, growling. Jordan gave a low commanding growl to his brother ordering him to stand down. Jordan obeyed, and the man laughed.

"Yes little doggy." he mocked. "You can tell your daddy that a hyena needs a word. The longer he keeps ignoring me, the longer I will drop bodies around this God-awful city."

Enraged, the shifter threw the girl almost 100 yards across the forest. The girl landed like a rag doll.

Jordan looked at the man and growled, *How dare you come on to my land and disrespect my pack.*

The man bellowed, "Fuck you and your pack!"

Jordan commanded his brothers to attack.

The man's bones cracked and reshaped. His neck swung, his arms, and legs reshaped, and within seconds he was a hyena.

Jacob came speeding out behind the tree about 50 yards, to his brother's 100 yards, away from the man. The man growled, upset with the fact that he let Jacob get so close without detection. He quickly weighed his odds, turned, and ran. *Chase* Jordan commanded. His brothers glanced at him quickly and spread apart among the forest, chasing the hyena.

The brothers stopped at the end of their property. It was a road, the only one that ran this far down here. One road in and one road out of the properties the pack owned. The three brothers turned around and ran back to the Alpha house.

Once on the balcony the brothers shifted all at the same time, returning them to their forms as men. They quickly dressed and Jordan said, "I will go to Dad's house. You two get your families home and safe, meet me there after." Jonathan and Jacob nodded and went back into the house through the accordion style doors.

Jordan got to his father's house and knocked on the door. His mother appeared smiling. Seeing his mother brought happiness to his heart. Diane was in her 50s, but looks 20 years younger. The only thing that gave her away is the grey hair pulled into a tight bun at the back of her head. She dyed her hair grey to fit in with the other woman her age to disguise the fact that she didn't age.

Mother wasn't born with the wolf; she was changed into a wolf. Only the Alpha has the power to change humans into wolves, or any shifter animal. This power was available for one night during the blood moon. Mom has been turned all of

Jordan's adult life. He really doesn't remember if she was or not when he was a kid.

His mother kissed him on the forehead and ushered him in the house. "My brothers are coming," he said.

Her brows creased. "All of my boys here at one time, that is never good." She placed her hand on her son's back and rubbed in little circles. "Anything I need to worry about?" she asked.

Jordan could not lie even if he wanted to, he wore his emotions on his sleeve. "I don't know Mom," Jordan said. "We just have to talk to Dad."

The crease became deeper. "Now, I don't know what is going on, I'll wait until we all sit together but Jordan, you know how your Father gets sometimes. I don't want you getting all worked up okay?" she took her thumb and ran it down the side of Jordan's face.

Jordan leaned into his mother's touch. "I love you Mom," Jordan said, ignoring the question. Jordan stood there a few more moments and then looked a step back. "Where's Dad anyway?" he asked.

She gave him a sharp look and then shook her head, "Your father is in the pool, doing laps," she said and then walked off.

Jordan went through the house towards the pool room. He passed family pictures on all the walls. One thing his mother was good for was capturing their precious and embarrassing moments and putting them on display for all to see.

He walked slowly down the hall looking at the pictures. Jordan didn't come over to his parents' house often. The bad blood between him and his father made things awkward. He couldn't expect his mother to choose between her children and her husband, so he stayed away.

Jordan got to the pool room door and hesitated as his hand

reached for the doorknob. He opened the door and walked in; his father was swimming laps.

Jordan took a deep breath. "Hello Father," he bellowed loud enough for him to hear. His father hesitated, but kept swimming. Jordan watched as his father finished swimming to the end of the pool and then turned around and headed back. Once he made it to the end of the pool, he got out and went over to get his towels.

"I don't have anything for you," his father said in his deep voice as he slowly dried himself off..

"We have questions for you, Father," Jordan said, not backing down.

John raised an eyebrow but didn't stop drying himself off. "Who is we?" he asked. "Okay, I have been worried enough. What is going on?" his mother asked hurriedly..

John finished drying off and began to walk out of the room. Jordan said quickly, "A hyena was on our property tonight and killed a woman. Told us to ask our Father why he was there."

All eyes turned towards John as he froze.

"John, you will not disrespect our son, our Alpha, this way. Turn to him and speak to him properly," Diane snapped.

"What is this about a hyena in Miami?"

John slowly turned and faced his son. John stood a few inches taller than Jordan and was more muscular. Jordan stood his ground, not breaking eye contact.

"What do you mean, killing women?" John said in a deep and hollow voice.

Jordan countered, "Who is the hyena?"

Diane spoke up, "John Romano what is going on? I am getting nervous listening to you."

John's face changed at his wife's voice. He took a couple steps towards his wife, ignoring his children completely. "There is nothing to worry about," he said.

Jordan spoke up again, "Tell me a story about the hyena."

John's face turned back to stone. Still looking at his wife, he began. "Sometime a few years ago, when I was Alpha," he growled. "We were trying to make an alliance with the hyena family in power over Africa. The Alpha's son was killed, and it was assumed that it was done by one of my wolves, since we were visiting, we got blamed."

Jacob spoke up, "I remember that trip, not the politics, but we left early without you and in a hurry."

John ignored his son and kept speaking to his wife. "I ended up getting into a fight with one of the hyena goons and won. Turns out he was another son of the Alpha."

Diane and ran her right hand softly down her husband's left cheek "So now it appears you killed two of the Alpha's sons," she said in a sympathetic voice.

"I got on a plane and flew home; I haven't heard anything from them since that trip." John said.

"What is their name, Father?" Jordan asked.

"Franklin's" John responded gruffly. He looked at his wife, and then turned and headed out of the room.

Jordan looked at his brothers as everyone exhaled from the tension. "So, is this hyena rouge or is the hyena family sending one of their own for revenge?"

Johnathan spoke up. "If they sent someone from their clan for revenge on our Father, why would the hyena come over here and kill innocent women?"

Diane looked at her sons in horror. "Women, as in plural?" she asked.

"Yes Mother," Jordan said softly. "The hyena told us that

there has been more than the one he left on our property."

"She is still out there now," Diane gasped and headed for the door, "I will go take care of it."

The brothers reacted with their shifter super speed. They blocked the door so that their mother could not leave.

She stopped and put her hands on her hips, scowling. "Now boys. I am a big girl; I can go clean up this mess. Show this girl some compassion."

The boys looked at each other as if debating. If they wanted to talk, they would have to do so verbally. Jordan nodded slightly, and his brothers made a path for his mother to pass. Once she left, they turned towards each other, standing in a circle.

"Jonathan, can you go into work and check out female homicides that have happened recently?" Jordan asked.

"Yea Detective Michaels" Jacob said, elbowing his brother.

Jonathan rolled his eyes. "Don't start on my last name, you know why I decided to take my wife's name instead of the other way around."

"Of course," Jacob mocked. "You can't protect your family. So, if anything were to happen to them because they are associated with the Romano's you wouldn't be able to forgive yourself."

Johnathan grabbed his brother by the shoulders and threw him 15 feet into the pool. "Because my wife wants to build her empire on her own and not with Romano connections," he yelled after his brother.

Jordan chuckled and put his hand on his brother's shoulder, shaking him back and forth slightly. "Why do you let him get to you every time Jonathan?" Jake said.

"It just pisses me off that he doesn't understand why I took Michaels."

Jordan chuckled again. "It's the wolf in you. Go check out those women, see what's happening with that and if the hyena was telling the truth."

"Got it," Johnathan said.

Connections

Jordan rolled over in his bed stretching, his arms and legs out wide. He rubbed his eyes and ran a hand through his hair. Going over to his window, he peeked through the blinds. Looking out on his territory he scanned slowly for any movement.

It has been almost two weeks since the hyena had come on to his property and this hiatus was unsettling. Taking off the shorts he wore to bed, Jordan opened the door in his bedroom that led to a private deck. Once on the deck he sniffed the air a few times. Nothing smelled foreign or out of place.

Jordan backed up, ran. and jumped over the balcony. Midair his bones started to crack, break, and reset. He went from two legs to four, and grew thick black fur. Trotting along his property, he inspected the surroundings.

He couldn't believe that girls got murdered on his property and he did not even notice it. How was he supposed to protect his pack if he couldn't even sense things happening? After surveying his property, he headed back to his house. He jumped back up on the balcony. When he landed, he shifted and was greeted by his sister Amara and his nephew Giovanni..

"Damn Jordan, put some clothes on," she exclaimed.

Jordan chuckled and rolled his eyes. He walked into his room and grabbed the shorts from on the floor where he left them and put them on. Amara stood, tapping her foot. Giovanni was looking everywhere else, but at his uncle's junk.

"What's up sis?" Jordan replied as he sat on the edge of his bed. Amara grabbed Giovanni by the arm and squeezed while dragging him, so he was closer to Jordan. First Giovanni didn't say anything. Behind him Amara growled, and Giovanni began to stutter.

"Uh- Uncle J - uh," then Amara gave him a hard shove in the back. Giovanni jerked forward and continued, "Uncle J, you know that girl who was found dead through the woods by here?"

Jordan looked at him quizzically, "Yes, and?"

"Well, I know who she is. Her name is Lisa, and she goes to my school. She was over at my house a few weeks ago."

"And what was she doing there?" she prompted.

Giovanni averting his eyes. "We had a party and invited her."

"The police just called and said they had proof that Giovanni invited her over to our house for a party the night she died. They had been sexting back and forth and Giovanni apparently was the last to see her alive," Amara yelled. "He attacked her Jordan. He raped her and sent her into the woods when we came early because you guys heard the hyena. He sent her into the woods after attacking her to fend for herself and the hyena found and killed her."

Jordan sat there confused. "So, they got into her phone, or pulled the records and saw that on the night she was murdered, Giovanni was the last person to see her alive," he repeated slowly, trying to process the information. "They seem to have a relationship according to the text messages they shared. So, it seems he was dating the girl, the last person to see her and then someone murdered her, is that correct?"

"He said -" Amara began but Jordan put one hand up. "Let him speak." he looked at Giovanni.

"We weren't dating. I was just trying to make her more comfortable with me, like me," Giovanni muttered and shrugged his shoulders.

"And why is that?" Jordan asked, standing now.

Giovanni hesitated and Jordan roared, "I am speaking to you!"

Giovanni jumped slightly, "Because I'm good with girls and I know they have to be comfortable and like me in order to come over."

Jordan was furious. Giovanni stared down at the floor feeling the Alpha power Jordan was radiating. Amara felt the same energy and involuntarily took a few steps back and lowered her head.

Giovanni put his head down slightly in deference to the Alpha power he was radiating. Jordan stared intently at Giovanni. "You brought another girl to my property to be played with," he spat venomously. "By you and your brothers. I hold you responsible for her murder and the pack will not be intervening in any police matters."

Giovanni's head shot up. Amara took a step forward and pleaded "Jordan, I know he needs to be punished, but this, this will ruin his life. Think about his future Jordan please."

"I will not explain or retract my decision." he said, his Alpha power radiating through the room.

Amara cried while Giovanni stood there with a blank look on his face. "Uncle J, that means I'm going to jail?" he asked.

"You will go through the criminal justice system like anyone else. You will need a lawyer, obtained through your parents' wealth, not the pack's wealth, or you will have a public defender.

You made it possible for a young girl to get murdered on my property because you and your brothers wanted to steal sex from her. That girl stood no chance with four human boys holding her down, let alone four wolf shifters. I've had enough of your reckless behavior, and your arrogance is insulting. Now, you deal with the consequences." Jordan turned around and went to his bathroom to shower.

Amara had tears streaming down her face. "Mom, you have to go talk to him," he said urgently, his hands gesturing towards the door.

Amara lifted her hand to put it on his cheek and stopped before she touched him. "The Alpha has spoken," she whispered fearfully. "Let's go tell your Father."

#

Jordan came from his shower and got dressed. When he was done, he grabbed his phone and saw he missed a message from Jonathan. Dialing, he put the phone to his ear and walked to the kitchen while it rang.

Jonathan: Hey Baby J, what's up?

Jordan: I am just returning your call. What's up with you?

Jonathan: I am at the house right now on my way out. I was wondering if you could come into the office with me and speak to my Captain.

Jordan: You and your Captain, for what?

Jonathan: I've got a lot to catch you up on.

Jordan: Gotcha' give me 30 minutes.

Jordan hung up the phone and put it on the counter, wondering what had happened. He had not spoken to his brother about the murdered girl, Lisa, since that night

Jordan shook his head, checked his phone and noticed he only had time for something quick to eat. Rummaging through the refrigerator, he heard his front door open and shut. It was his mother. She smelled like mango, whatever soap or perfume she used left a slight mango smell that he hated when he was younger but learned to love.

Diane lightly padded through the house silently. Jordan sighed heavily. He didn't have time to go through this with his mother, not right now. As Alpha he didn't have to explain anything to anyone. That included his mother, but he would always be her baby, whether he liked it or not. Jordan pulled leftover hamburger patties out of the fridge and popped him in the microwave when his mother walked into the kitchen. Jordan stopped and faced her.

"Hello Mother," he said with a smile.

"What is this your sister is telling me about?" she asked.

"Mom, the pack will not cover for him. I am on my way to meet Johnathan now. I will tell him what has happened and what my orders are," he explained..

Diane looked at him with hurt eyes. "I know your nephew has made some mistakes-"

Jordan's anger rose and all he heard was his rage. "Mother," he said slowly, trying to keep his emotions in check. "He has raped multiple girls. He has made the same mistake over and repeatedly. Because of his bad decision making, and sense of superiority he has violated and humiliated countless girls. They are not mistaking Mother, and this pack is done financing and covering his bad decisions."

"The family will be humiliated, Jordan," she said. "The reason we look out for each other is so that we don't get humiliated in public. You need to help your sister and your nephew," She calmly walked towards him and raised her arms.

Jordan stood there looking at her, "I did not ask for your

opinion Mother. My decision is made and will not be retracted. Amara and her husband will be the only ones allowed to give anything besides emotional support to Giovanni."

Diane froze and stared at her son. "Jordan."

Jordan interrupted her, "No, Mother this discussion is over."

Diane scowled, staring up at him, not breaking eye contact. "Yes, Alpha," she said and then walked out of the kitchen. A few moments later he heard the front door open and close. Jordan leaned against the counter and rubbed his hand down his face.

The microwave beeped, and he jerked his head. He had forgotten about the food, but he couldn't get it now. He had to get on the road if he was going to be on time to meet Jonathan. Jordan grabbed his phone and looked at the screen as he was walking towards the front door. There were multiple missed calls and messages he was not going to check. Jordan grabbed his keys from the side of the door and headed to his car.

Combining two worlds

Jordan parked in the MDPD visitors' parking lot. He entered the building and went to the receptionist sitting behind a glass partition. It reminded him of going to the bank; the tellers standing behind the glass. Jordan smiled and read her name tag.

"Hello, Miranda. My name is Jordan Romano. I am here to see detective Jonathan Michael; he is expecting me."

Miranda nodded. "One second please" and then started typing on her computer. A few moments later she picked up the phone sitting next to her and made a call. Jordan listened to her say his name and then a few "Okay's" and "Yes Sir's." She hung up the phone and smiled up at him. "You can head up to the 3rd floor sir."

Jordan thanked her and headed to the elevator doors. Once the elevator doors opened Jonathan was standing there, waiting for him.

"Hey BJ" short for Baby Jordan. Jordan got off the elevator and followed his brother down the hall.

"What is all of this with Giovanni?" Jonathan asked.

"He raped the same girl that the hyena murdered that night," Jordan whispered.

Jonathan ushered Jordan into an office and gestured for him to sit down. "Wait, you mean the girl who was in the woods was out there hanging with Giovanni?"

"He invited her over and raped her and threw her over the balcony. She went stumbling through the woods-"

"And the hyena killed her," Jonathan finished. He sat there with his hand on his chin, letting the information process. Finally, he said, "And you don't want me to try to help Giovanni?"

Jordan shook his head. "Not this time. We have always helped him in the past, and he keeps doing this repeatedly. This time Amara, Steve, and Giovanni are on their own. So, what is going on, why am I here?"

Jonathan was silent for a few moments and then switched gears. "I had the database search for females killed with slashes or animal teeth marks."

Jordan sat up straighter in his chair. "And?"

"There have been six women over the past six months murdered by what was described as claw marks or with what looks like animal teeth marks. I asked my Captain who was working these cases, and he asked why I was interested. After a conversation, he told me that there was a multi-agency special investigations division who investigate crimes committed by the city's shifters."

Jordan looked at his brother with surprise. "You're telling me that there is a team of police officers who not only know that there are shifters but investigate them and what? Do they just arrest them? No jail would hold shifters." Jordan asked.

"Apparently yes," Johnathan said. "I put in a request. The team is only made up of two people right now. One I just worked on a case with, her name is Jelena Cohert. She is a Senior Agent in the FBI. There is another officer named Peter Macwell who works in patrol. He is a veteran and has been there for 20-plus years."

Jordan's interest was piqued now. "How is she in the FBI working cases with you and also hunting shifters at the same time?" he asked.

"They aren't hunting shifters. When someone is murdered, and it looks like it was done by an animal they get called in to investigate. They do their day jobs the rest of the time."

"You want to join this team, so why am I here?" Jordan asked.

"I told my Captain that my Alpha would consult on this one," Johnathan grinned. "So come on Alpha, let's go consult."

#

María was sitting in her father's office, pleading. "Papí please, he is hitting me. We fight each other, punching and kicking. I should not have to fight my husband. Everything makes him mad. I love my job and do not like to gear up for a fight every time I come in the house late."

"¡Basta María!"<Enough Maria!> Her father yelled. "You're exaggerating, you two do not fight each other." Her father waved a hand dismissively. "I need you to stop coming here making up this nonsense. Now you have a case right, a family you are working with. Do you need help with your case?"

María looked at her father, hurt and blinked a few times to stop herself from crying. fHer Father looked at her with impatience. "Nunca volveré a hablar contigo."<I will never speak to you again> She stood up , anger boiling inside of her. "I have come to you and Oliver asking for help. I come to my father and my brother and all I seem to get is Mr. Dominguez and Mr. Monroe. So, from this point on I will only deal with either one of you in that capacity." She waited for him to respond. Mr. Dominguez looked at her stonily e and redirected his attention towards his computer.

María would never allow him the satisfaction of seeing her cry. She whipped around and left the office. On her way out of the building she prayed she didn't see anyone. She couldn't bear letting anyone here see her cry.

Arriving at her car she put her head down in her arms, sobbing silently until she did not have anything left inside her. Picking up her head, she pulled a tissue from the glove box and wiped her face. Taking a deep breath María headed out.

When she arrived home, she put her things in the proper places and went straight into the kitchen to begin preparing dinner. She wasn't late coming home, but she would have normally been home 20 minutes earlier. She rushed into the kitchen and spotted Alejandro standing there, leaning against the countertop, she stopped in her tracks.

"¿Dónde has estado?"<Where have you been?> He asked.

Jelena looked at him nervously. That familiar pit growing in her stomach. Her palms began sweating, her heart started beating quicker. Her fight-or-flight response was kicking in, and with Alejandro fight was always the only option. "I was at work," she replied calmly.

"Your work," he began. "Or your father's work?"

Maria's rage flared instantly. How dare her father call him and tell him where she was and what she was doing? She felt betrayed, angry but most of all hurt. "I stopped by my Father's office after work," she told him.

Alejandro advanced on her, walking slowly across the room until they were mere inches apart. María focused on keeping her breathing even and made sure she didn't look Alejandro in the eye, that made him mad. Looking as if you weren't paying attention made him mad too though.

"And what did you tell your father?" he asked menacingly..

"We both know you talked to my father, why are we playing this game?" she asked. The next moment a hard, powerful slap came across her left cheek knocking off balance and she stumbled slightly. She tried to reclaim her balance so she could prepare for the next hit, there was always another hit. She wasn't quick enough this time. Before she could firmly plant her feet on the ground, three more slaps sent her falling towards the floor.

"Who do you think you are talking to?" He bellowed. "Get up," he continued. "Don't act like a victim now. Come on, fight back," he said waving his hands in a 'come here' motion.

María put one hand on each side of her face. Her cheeks stung from the multiple hits and her pride hurt. She tried to re-orient herself to get up, but she struggled. She looked up and seen a closed fist coming at her–

\#

The elevator dinged, and the door opened, shaking Cohert out of her daydreaming. Cohert got out of the elevator and went to her office. She had not been in the bureau building for two weeks and she missed it. She had spent a lot of years in the FBI and had never spent this much time out of work. She was eager to get back into the office and check emails, see what her team was doing. Cohert checked her watch and then left to go to Monroe's office.

When she arrived, she saw Monroe, Cross, Macwell, Michaels, and another gentlemen standing around talking. She entered, and all eyes turned towards her. Cross and Michaels had smiles plastered on their faces.

"Damn girl," Cross said. "Look at you. Let me see you do this." He raised his arms over his head and bent at the waist from side to side. The room laughed. Michaels said, "Lift your shirt, I need to see." He saw the room staring at him. "The scars, I mean the scars keep your minds out of the gutter."

"Yeah, I'm good, I'm back" Cohert did a few jumping jacks and threw a few punches. She crossed the room and hugged Cross and Michaels. She gave Macwell a firm handshake and then turned and looked at Oliver. They looked at each other awkwardly and then nodded. He has been there for her with her injuries and with Dan the past few weeks, but it was different behavior than she was used to.

Angela said she just didn't give him a chance to be the big brother. She told Angela she did, and he blew it. Angela countered by saying that she holds a grudge for too long and it was about time she got over it. Cohert looked at Jordan and stuck her hand out. "I don't think we've met" she said, "I'm Jelena Cohert."

Jordan looked at her intently, his senses picking up the light smell of vanilla, the soothing rhythmic beating of her heart, the dilation of her pupils. He felt something deep in his gut, a feeling he has never felt before. He grabbed her hand. "I'm Jordan Romano," he said in a low voice. "I am Michael's baby brother." Cohert's head jerked back slightly and Macwell said, "I'll be damned."

Jordan held on to her hand for longer than he should have. He heard his brother chuckle in the background and then finally let her go.

"Why the hell isn't your last name Romano?" Macwell grunted..

Michaels signed and rolled his eyes while Jordan chuckled. "It is a story he hates to tell." Jordan said.

"I took my wife's last name," Michaels finally said.

Cross looked at him in amusement, "Even I don't know this story, come out with it."

Michaels signed again. "My wife wanted to build her career without the backing of the Romano name. So instead of her taking my last name, I took hers. It was still important that me, he,r and our kids have the same last name," He said in one big breath.

"It has been brought to our attention that we have another victim of what's been happening the past six months. This makes the seventh victim. I know Highworth and then Kinkcade has had our focus recently but now I need the three of you, to switch gears. Jordan is the Alpha of the Romano pack and the leader of the North American sector," Monroe said.

Cohort glanced over at him only to find he was already staring at her with eyes like he wanted to eat her. *Hell, he is a damn wolf,* she thought, *he probably does want to eat me.*

"Can I get the rundown on that one?" Cohert asked. "Has the crime scene been preserved, were the techs called out?"

Jordan's eyes turned hard. "We did not preserve the crime scene. We didn't know it was a crime scene initially. I can't even tell you what happened to the body."

"Why not?" Cohert glared at him.

Michaels jumped in. "Our Mother took care of it. We have a family thing going on with some hyenas. We didn't know Lisa was connected to any murders happening here. I didn't even know about the murders happening here."

"You know her name," she accused suspiciously.

Michaels looked at Jordan for permission and Cohert wanted to snap her fingers to make him look at her. She knew the pack hierarchy and he couldn't speak on pack business without Alpha permission.

She stood there, growing impatient waiting for Jordan to decide.

"Apúrate" she grumbled. Oliver gave her a hard look, and she rolled her eyes. Turning towards Jordan, she stepped into his space, breaking the eye contact between him and his brother.

"Look," she began. "I understand the pack rules, I have been doing this long enough, but we don't have the space for secrets. I can promise you your business won't leave this room; I can promise to be discreet to the best of my ability. I can even promise to not let people know you are here and in what capacity. What I can't and won't tolerate is anyone obstructing my investigation."

Jordan's eyes flared. She stared at him trying to identify the emotion in his eyes. She assumed it would be anger, because she challenged him, but it wasn't.

His lust was bubbling behind the surface. He loved how she spoke to him matter-of-factly without being scared, but still being respectful. He looked at Michaels and lifted his chin.

Cohert brought her attention back to Michaels, and he said "Our nephew Giovanni -"

"Giovanni Romano?" Macwell interrupted incredulously. "With all due respect that kid is a low life predator."

Michaels and Jordan both growled and Macwell held up his hands in a surrender motion with his palms facing out. "Hey, Listen. I don't mean any harm, but that kid has raped girls and I know that y'all know it because y'all helped him out of his mess each time."

"We have a code," Jordan began evenly. "We help our family. It was better for our family that Giovanni's stupid decisions do not make it into the news. This time, he will follow the rules of the criminal justice system as any other teenager would."

"What happened this time? Isn't it still in your family's best interest to stay out of the news?" Cohert questioned.

Jordan looked at Michaels so he could continue. "He invited Lisa, don't know her last name, over to their house a few weeks ago so he could force sexual intercourse. That is the same night we had an issue on the property, so we sent all the pack members back to their houses. Everyone was hanging out at Jordan's. Giovanni's parents came home earlier than he expected, and he threw the girl out. She went running into the woods surrounding our house to get away where a hyena was waiting for us, but so happened to come across her and killed her to make his point."

"So," Cohert said, processing the information. "The only reason our latest victim, Lisa–"

"Hemmingway," Monroe filled in.

"Was in a position to be killed is because your nephew was trying to *rape* her?" Cohert continued, looking at Michaels making her point that she caught his vocabulary change. "Here is another unrelated question. How many times have you gotten your nephew off rape charges?"

Anger erupted in Jordan, and he pushed Alpha power through the room. Michaels took an involuntary step back and lowered his head. However, he was the only shifter in the room and therefore the only one who felt the rush of power to the full extent.

Macwell adjusted his jacket and a feeling of unidentified threat had come over him. Cross's head shot up and he began looking around as if someone else was in the room. Cohert got into her protective stance. Monroe, not feeling anything different, went rigid when he saw Cohert's body change. He saw her looking intently at Jordan.

"Did I hurt your feelings?" she said slyly.

Jordan took a step forward, causing Cohert to mimic the

movement in reverse.

Monroe slammed his fist on his desk. "We will stay professional here. Whatever mojo you just threw out that has got everyone on edge, cut it out. Secondly, that's my sister and I do not play when it comes to my sister."

"Sister!" Macwell barked out and rubbed his hands through his short brown hair. "Let me get this straight. This one took his wife's last name and is really a Romano of the Romano packs," he pointed a finger at Michaels. "And you two are brother and sister. Any more secrets, ya' know I hate being left out of the loop."

"Macwell calm down," Cohert said. "The fact that Monroe is my brother is not something I would like getting around. It is on a need to know basis. And frankly I don't think Jordan here needed to know," she scowled at her brother. "Now, back to the matter at hand."

Cohert looked at Jordan, "Don't worry, we'll talk about your nephew later," and turned her attention to Monroe.

Monroe kept his eyes trained on Jordan. Jordan looked from Cohert to Monroe and nodded his head while lifting his hands slightly, silently apologizing. Jordan knew the man couldn't take him on, but he also understood the need to protect his sister, so he let it go. Monroe started speaking to the group again, but Jordan wasn't paying attention, he was looking at Cohert.

Jordan let the name Jelena Cohert swirl around in his head a few times. He didn't know what it was about her, but he was ready and willing to find out. Tuning everyone else out, he stared from the head and glazed over her body until he landed on her shoes. *Yeah*, he thought, this was something he had to pursue.

"I have medical examiner reports and things there, but we also would need to catch Michaels up to speed on the last six murders. We have Michaels and Jordan's help and that should make this case easier to solve with the inside help. When the suspect is found and captured, he will be turned over to SIDDU which is the Special Investigations Division detention immediately. I need you all to go get your SID gear and make sure you have new models on everything. Time to get back in SID mode. Michaels, I know you don't need gear, but you are required to have it to keep up appearances. Cross is taking over for Ferriety, he retired so we are your contact." Monroe finished and waited to see if there were any questions.

Macwell spoke up, "How do we know you two won't be sharing secret information. I mean, you are brother and sister after all."

"Enough," Cohert sighed. "I don't have the patience for you to be overdramatic. We have been siblings this whole time."

Monroe interrupted, "Since there are no questions you all can get to it." The room disbursed in chatter and Monroe pulled Cohert aside. "Hey, have you taken your psychological eval yet?" he asked.

"Yes," she rolled her eyes. "I am not crazy and cleared for duty."

"Okay, then I need you to meet with Angela and Belle on Kinkcade. Bell, Jonathan, and Spearmen are working on High-worth, as well as something new. They need to get you up to date. Once you've met with them tell them their boss is back and to leave me alone." he chuckled..

Cohert rolled her eyes again. Monroe told everyone to go use Cohert's office and get out of his. As they were walking down the hall Cohert suggested, "Let's go down and gear up first."

"Do I have gear?" Jordan asked playfully, as they began walking towards the basement Jordan.

"You don't need any gear," she said, returning his playfulness. "Or are there some parts that are not working that you need to protect?"

"All of my parts are working, I just felt left out," Jordan chuckled.

"Stop flirting and let's focus on the job," Macwell said.

"I know we haven't seen each other in a while Macwell," Cohert began. "But you are really starting to irritate me. I need you to chill out."

"Or what, you'll get your brother on me," he replied.

Cohert stopped in her tracks and turned, facing Macwell. She took a few steps forward, so she was in his face. "By the time I get done with you, there won't be anything left for my brother. Now unless you want to be reassigned and replaced, I figure it is time for you to not speak unless spoken to."

"The way I hear it, making threats is what got you almost killed in the first place," Macwell replied.

"The way I hear it," Cohert hissed. "You can return to your patrol. Your services are no longer needed." She turned on her heels and walked away.

Jordan stood, stunned. Michaels nudged him as he walked by. "When she walks away, we follow," he said and then followed.

Once in the gear room Cohert, felt her phone buzzing. She took it out of her pocket and looked at the caller ID. Seeing it was Monroe she almost didn't pick up, but she was professional. *Since when do I struggle with staying professional with Monroe? She thought.*

Cohert: Yes?

Monroe: He is debriefing, do you need another body?

Cohert: We don't have enough time to break someone else in. I will use Jordan.

They hung up just as Michaels and Jordan walked into the room. "You'll use Jordan for what?" Jordan asked, lifting his right eyebrow

"Cálmate, '' she said, patting his chest. "I was talking about work. You are my third body since Macwell will no longer be with us."

Jordan put his right hand to his forehead in a solute motion. "Yes sir," he said.

Cohert rolled her eyes "Okay so," she said, picking up a gear bag and emptying its contents onto a table. She began explaining the use of each item she pulled out. "We have your regular guns with silver bullets. We only use silver bullets; well I will only use silver bullets." She shrugged .

"Next we have this necklace," she held up a simple gold chain. "This interrupts the telepathy that shifters have. If I wear it and you are within 500 feet of me, you two will not be able to communicate telepathically with each other. That's where these come in," she said holding up what looked like stud earrings. "These are basically 'coms' but they can only communicate with the 'coms' that come in the set. There are four in this set. We will only use three and the fourth one will go to Monroe and Cross."

"The last thing," she said, pulling out what looked like a bullet-proof vest. "This helps me mostly, with being attacked by claws and sharp teeth. The material is hard to slice through. So, I will still get hurt, but I won't get shredded to pieces."

Jordan looked at her skeptically. "So you're saying that these will stop claws?"

"Not stop completely. It will make it harder to just rip and slash. So, I will still get hurt, just not as bad." Cohert noticed he was still skeptical. "You want to try it out?"

His eyes widened a fraction, and he raised his eyebrow "What do you mean, try it out?"

"Well, I am not putting the thing on," she laughed. "Shift and swipe at it so you know what I mean."

Michaels started coughing and Jordan just stared at her in amazement. "You want me to shift?" he asked her.

"Uhh, do we think that is a good idea?" Michaels asked, catching his breath.

"I am fine with it if she is fine with it," he smirked, unbuttoning his belt and slipping his feet out of his shoes.

Michaels put his hands up in a stop motion. "Hold on, we are in the FBI building. Do we really believe that shifting is a good idea?" Jordan continued as if Michaels had not spoken. He finished unhooking his belt and fumbled with the button and zipper. Not taking his eyes off her, still smirking, he pulled at his jeans and let them hit the floor.

He still had his boxers on, but Cohert knew that those had to go too. When a shifter shifted, all these clothes shredded to pieces. She was trying to appear unimpressed. Jordan began to unbutton his shirt and let it slide off his arms and hit the floor. *Is he trying to do a striptease?* This made her giggle, and Jordan's smirk turned into a cocky chuckle.

She hadn't noticed his broad shoulders and chiseled chest beneath his tank top. *Well, not until just now* she thought. He took the tank top from the bottom and lifted it up and over his head.

"Okay," Michaels interrupted irritated. "If you are going to make this stupid decision, hurry up and stop making it a striptease."

Jordan cut a side glance at Michaels and growled.

"Oh, stop it!" Cohert exclaimed. "Michaels has a point, stop feeling yourself and hurry up."

Jordan's eyes flashed with irritation. "Stand back a little. Remember, I won't hurt you so don't be scared."

Cohert scoffed and rolled her eyes. Jordan took that as a challenge. In one moment, he was Jordan standing in his boxers, the next she heard terrible bone cracking. Before she could get over that horrible sound, a large black wolf was standing in front of her. She had seen plenty of shifter animals, but they always amazed her.

Jordan telepathically told Michaels to let her know to hold up the vest.

"Hey," Michaels said, grabbing Cohert's attention. She turned her head slowly, her eyes not leaving Jordan until the last possible minute. Finally, looking at Michaels. she said "Huh?"

"Hold up the vest," Michaels said.

Cohert snapped out of her stupor and held up the vest. "Come on, hurry up" she said.

Jordan stepped forward and lifted his huge paw up in the air telling Michaels *"Tell her not to be scared. I won't hurt her."*

Michaels looked at her, "He said hold still."

Cohert rolled her eyes, knowing that is not what Jordan said. Jordan stepped forward and sat on his hind legs. He took his paw and swiped at the vest. It ripped through but when he went to drag his paw, it would not budge. He struggled with the material a little and then told Michaels to have her let it go.

Cohert let the material go and Jordan let it drop to the floor. Jordan then placed one paw on top of it, holding it in place, and continued to swipe with the right paw. Cohert knew he wasn't going to give up.

"Cambio," she said, instructing him to change back into his human form.

Jordan obeyed and Cohert watched in amazement as the horrible sound of bones cracking led to a wolf turning into a man right in front of her. Jordan stood up and stretched his neck slightly from side to side, completely naked, since the change shredded the boxers.. Distracted by the vest, he picked it up off the floor. He held it up inspecting the incisions., "I couldn't tear it," he said, looking at Michaels.

Michaels reached for the vest and then realized Jordan was still naked. "Put your clothes back on," he groaned as he took the vest to inspect it. Jordan smirked as he realized that he was naked in front of Cohert. Shifters didn't like seeing each other naked, but it came with the territory. You were always respectful and put your clothes on as soon as possible.

There were exceptions though; some situations where that wasn't possible or times where you got distracted and forgot. Jordan picked up his pants and stepped into them. He was looking at Cohert, who seemed engrossed in her phone. This made him chuckle. She looked up at him just as he was pulling his jeans over his hips.

"What's so funny?" she asked him.

"You," he said in a low voice, daring her to challenge him.

Instead, she turned to Michaels. "What do you think?"

"I see the holes; I can't imagine that Jordan couldn't swipe through though." he said.

"No, I was trying," Jordan jumped in. "Especially when she dropped it and I had it on the floor. I could not get it to rip. What is it made of?"

"I actually don't know," she shrugged. "I just make sure it works; I don't ask extra questions."

Jordan looked from Michaels to Cohert. "It really wouldn't let me rip through though, only punctured." Jordan finished putting these clothes on."Okay, so what's next?"

"Each of us gets a bag," Cohert began. "I will go get tablets and put all the case files on them before you leave. Let's give each other a day or so to become familiar and then meet up and compare notes."

"Okay, so meet the day after tomorrow at your place or your second house?" Michaels asked.

Cohert hesitated., Michaels caught on, "Or not?"

"I am staying with Rodriguez for right now," she began. "The bureau took possession of the second house per my request."

Jordan jumped in, when he noticed her shifting her weight from side to side and he heard her heart speed up. "How about my place? Give me your number and I will text you the details," he said as he unlocked his phone and handed it to her.

To Cohert, it seemed like the best option. She took his phone and began typing in her number when she heard Michaels chuckle. Her fingers froze a little, and she realized maybe he had ulterior motives for wanting her number. He had been flirting with her the whole time. She finished adding her number and handed him his phone back.

"The day after tomorrow?" Jordan asked, looking at Cohert.

"Yup," she said cheerfully, "just text me."

Each of them took one of the bags with gear in it and left the room.

Back to work

C ohert was in her office clicking through emails when her phone buzzed. She glanced and saw it was a text message and ignored the phone.

She had so much work she had to do. The boring part of the job was paperwork, approving, and denying requests. Reading through case files. The list went on and on; and because she had been out for so long her list was three times the size as others. Her computer beeped, and a message popped up in the lower right corner. It said 'Relator' and cursed herself for forgetting.

Looking at her phone she saw the message was from her father reminding her about their open house today. She was glad she had her phone calendar hooked up to her computer and vice versa or she would have never checked her phone and missed the appointment with her father. He irritated her sometimes.

There was no reasoning with him when his mind was set. He was still intent about having her budget at $350,000 and putting a down payment of 25%. She finally had the chance to look through her finances and she knew for sure she couldn't afford that. She had always saved and done well for herself. When she separated her money from Dan, she was generous and left more than she should have. She did not want to give him any reason to become crazier.

With a sigh, she closed her computer and gathered her things. She exited her office, awaiting to hear the door click behind her.

Opening the door to Angela's apartment and dropping her stuff on the couch she checked the time on the wall. She had just enough time to freshen up slightlys.

She was headed to a rural area, on the outskirts of Miami. Ms. Bullyums told her there was more wilderness than people. She had to admit the idea of living far away from the city. That is one thing she liked about living in the suburbs. After a day at work she couldn't wait to get back to a slower pace. She imagined living in a rural area, away from Dan, would be even better. The thought made her shiver and shame settled in the pit of her stomach.

She went into the bathroom connected to Angela's bedroom. She washed her face and put her moisturizer, on followed by mascara. After brushing her teeth, she quickly put her hair into a ponytail, gathered her things, and left the apartment.

#

Jelena arrived at the open house 45 minutes later. On her drive she pondered whether she would want to drive this distance every day. She parked the car and was about to text her Father when someone knocked at the window

"Date prisa, hija,"<Hurry up, daughter> her father said.. With a sigh, she gathered her things and then got out of the car.

Jelena was in awe of the house. It was a beautiful colonial style home. The landscaping was nice, and trim compared to the forest vibe that surrounded the property. She loved the short hedges that ran along the long driveway. As she and her father walked on the path that was parallel to the driveway, she spotted a fountain up ahead.

As they got closer, the fountain was surrounded by beautiful flowers hugging the outside and a lovely stone pattern that transitioned from the gravel driveway perfectly. The stone was wide enough for a car to drive up here and park directly in front of the house. Past the fountain, the stone continued and led to a small pathway and stairs leading up the gorgeous house.

Ms. Bullyums was happily standing at the doorway. "Hello guys," she said waving widely. Jelena and her father approached. Jelena greeted her warmly and then glanced at her father who still looked stern.

"Come on in," she said, gesturing wildly again with her hand.

The three of them entered the house and Ms. Bullyums went on with her script. Jelena was not paying attention though. Her breath caught as soon as she walked into the house.

The entryway was grand. There was a double staircase directly ahead of the doorway. Everything was modern rustic. She loved the wood accents. Past the entryway there was a grand formal living room. The house was staged and whoever did the decorating had a beautiful eye. Everything was gorgeous and went well together. To one side of the space was a doorway leading to what looked like a kitchen and to the other side which looked like some type of room with large lounge chairs set up.

Jelena stopped abruptly because she bumped into her father who was stopped.

"Presta atención," he barked. Jelena scowled slightly and then turned her attention to Ms. Bullyums.

"Okay, enough of my talking. Go ahead and explore then meet me here when you are done, and we will chat," she chirped..

Jelena looked at her father, and he nudged her. She turned

and walked into the room to the left first. There was a big screen at the front of the room with six large reclinable lounge chairs. *They have cup holders* she thought to herself in amazement. *It's a movie theater; this house has a movie theater.* "There is no way I can afford this," she muttered aloud.

She left the media room and crossed the formal living room to the room on the opposite end. She walked into a large kitchen and marveled at the design. There were wood columns on the ceilings going the length of the room.

She stopped at a large simple white island with a cooktop to the left and a dishwasher to the right, hidden. There were three stools on the opposite side. The cabinets were all along one wall and had a wood trim with glass inserts. The oven and microwave were below the upper cabinets, embedded in the lower ones.

Jelena continued her tour and walked from the open kitchen space to a large dining room. There was a table where eight could fit comfortably. There were pictures and paintings on the wall, but Jelena guessed they were just for show and paid then no attention.

The dining room, which was open to the kitchen, was also open to another living space. This one had a tv mounted over the fireplace. It had a sectional and three reclining chairs. Underneath the coffee table was a bright-colored area rug that she loved. The room was set up with fewer lamps and plants than the living space in the front of the house. Jelena figured that was because this one was more lived in.

After Jelena wandered around upstairs, she met her father and Ms. Bullyums back in the front room.

"So Mrs. Cohert, what do you think?" Ms. Bullyums enthused. "Call me Jelena please," she said. "This house is amazing. I love the staging and everything."

"Okay," Bullyums began. "This is a different situation. This house is on Romano land. They want to lease the property, not sell it. They want $1,500 a month but all other utilities, including maintenance of the grounds are included. If you want to move, you just give them the 30 day notice you would give any other landlord."

"Did you say Romano land?" Jelena asked, barely hearing anything she said after that.

Ms. Bullyums smiled "Yes. I caught on that you are in some type of transitional period in your life and you were a little overwhelmed with your father's, uh, suggestions," she said, looking nervously from Jelena to her father and back again. "I was looking through my catalogue at what options I had and this one stuck out. It has been available for quite some time though. I cannot find anyone who wants to lease."

Just then they heard a "Erica dear, are you in here?"

Bullyums replied, "In the front room." She turned towards Jelena and her father "This is wonderful, I would like you two to meet Diane Romano." A well put together lady walked from the back of the house with a grand smile on her face. She immediately walked up to Jelena and her father sticking her hand out. "I am Diane Romano," she said, "and you must be?"

Jelena stumbled over her words for a minute while she grabbed her hand in return. Mr. Dominguez introduced himself and Jelena. Diane turned around and kissed Ms. Bullyums twice, once on each cheek. She turned and clasped her hands together in front of her. "Did we do the tour?"

"The house is gorgeous," Jelena said, finally after finding her voice.

"We are asking for $1,500 a month. That will be your only

bill, we cover everything else. We are so excited to get someone here. It's been ages. Now it ultimately is up to my son, but we don't have that many candidates. And between me and you," she said leaning towards them cospiratorily. "You are the one with the most promise."

Jelena chuckled. "I'm going to have to text him and threaten him to give me the place."

Diane and her father looked at her curiously. "You know my son?" she asked.

"I work with Michaels, err, Jonathan. I just met Jordan recently through him." Jelena said, silently cursing herself for not thinking before she spoke.

"Hmm," Diane said. "Do you mind taking a walk with me through the backyard Jelena? It is the best feature of the house."

Jelena nodded and agreed, then followed Diane through to the back of the house. Next to the refrigerator in the kitchen. there were accordion style doors. Diane opened them and stepped outside. Without looking at Jelena she said, "It is a little concerning to me that you know, one I had more than one son and secondly which one I was speaking about when I said I needed to consult him first."

"Ma'am, your family has quite the reputation around here. It was a joke I didn't think through completely, I should have kept it to myself." She rushed out hoping to do some damage control.

"Your joke doesn't concern me," Diane said. "What I believe you know does." Diane looked at her directly in the eye.

"Ma'am," Jelena started. "The only thing I know about you is what the papers and the media say. I just got off a case with Michaels, and when you work with someone you get close. That's how I know he has a brother named Jordan."

"Jonathan's name is not Romano," Diane shot back.

"We worked closely together," Jelena countered. "If you still are interested in me living here, I would love to take it. The leasing and ease of other utilities is perfect for my current situation, plus the house is beautiful." Jelena gestured while keeping eye contact with Diane.

"Give me two business days," Diane began. "I will get back to you." With that she turned and went back into the house.

Hey renter

J ordan sat in front of the TV in his house, accompanied by his siblings for the weekly movie night. Every week they sat down and watched a movie together just them. No kids, cousins or parents. They were watching something on Netflix, although Jordan wasn't paying attention.

All he could think about was Jelena. *Where on earth had this girl come from*, he thought. Yesterday was the last time he had seen her but it felt like an eternity. Still daydreaming, he did not notice when his mother walked in. She tapped him on the shoulder and bent down to whisper in his ear "Come here, please."

Shaken out of his stupor he got up and went to follow his mother. Once in the kitchen she laid the four candidate folders on the table. "These are my top three choices to move into the house down on the edge of property." She purposefully placed Jelena's folder last in the row.

Jordan walked over and began flipping through the folders, mainly looking at the attached headshots. "You know Mother," he began. "I really don't care who you put in the house." He froze on the last folder when flipped open Jelena's picture. Jordan picked up the folder and closely reviewed its contents, something he did not do with the last three folders.

"Who is this girl?" Diane asked. "I met her today, and she knew Jonathan and you."

"She gets the house and all the things that are staged." He closed the folder and placed it on the table. Then looked up at his mother.

"Who is this girl?" Diane asked again, looking at her son.

"She works with Jonathan; I know her through him," he stated, with a look that told her the conversation was over.

Diane looked at him for a few more moments, and picked up the folders. "I will make the call first thing in the morning." She turned and walked away.

Back in front of the television with his siblings, Jordan pulled out his phone to text Jelena. He opened the message section of his phone and typed her name in. Staring at the phone he typed *'hey'* and then erased it. Then he typed *'how are you?'* and then erased it. For a third time he typed in *'is this Agent Cohert?'* and then erased it again.

His siblings laughed at the movie and he looked up, chuckling to make it seem like he was paying attention. Finally, he texted *'Hey renter'* and sent it before he lost his nerve and erased it again. He stared at his phone and waited for her to text back. His siblings laughed again, and he put his phone down.

I am not going to stare at my phone waiting, he thought. Jordan got into the movie and forgot about the text message.

After the movie everyone went home, and Jordan headed upstairs to shower. He took his phone out of his pants before shooting them in the basket. Looking at his phone he saw a message. Jordan smiled from ear to ear when he read Jelena's reply '*so that means I got it?*' He went to text her back immediately, but didn't want to seem too eager. Placing his phone on the bed, he got in the shower.

Sometime later, Jordan came rushing out of the bathroom. He picked up his phone and typed '*You knew I would give it to you*'.

She replied immediately saying '*Your mother didn't seem to like me very much, so I was concerned.*' Jordan laughed out loud '*It was never my mother's decision.*' As he sat there watching his phone waiting for a reply, he hit the call button. Before he had the chance to change his mind, he heard hello over the line. He sat on his bed in his towel and spoke on the phone with Jelena for hours. They talked about everything from house details to favorite movies. Jordan was lying on his bed when he let out a hearty laugh.

"So you like love stories?"

Jelena scoffed, "Sandra Bullock does other genres besides romance."

"She does, name one?" Jordan countered.

Jelena was silent while she thought. "Aha see," Jordan chimed in. "You can't!"

"Shhh," Jelena said. "What about Bird Box?"

"That is a love story," Jordan said and then went on to justify his opinion to her.

When he was finished Jelena clicked her tongue. "You make a strong argument. What about Ocean's 8?"

Jordan took a minute to think. "I wouldn't say romance but definitely a chick flick."

"Esperar," Jelena said. "You said nothing about chick flicks. You said romance."

"Es-per-roar," Jordan said, butchering it. "What does that

mean?"

Jelena giggled. "First of all that is not how you say it. It is pronounced ehs-peh-rahr, and it means to hold on or to wait."

Jordan tried saying it again, but how Jelena said it. After explaining to him he had to roll his tongue, he caught on. They spent the next few minutes going over basic Spanish.. His phone beeped; it was his mother. He thought about ignoring her, but decided to click over and tell her he was on the phone.

When he told Jelena to hold and clicked over. all he heard his mother say was 'under attack.' Jordan dropped his phone and threw off the towel. Heading to his balcony he pushed on the doors and jumped over. When he hit the ground, he was the majestic black wolf.

\#

He took a second, opening his senses fully to inspect his property. He smelled his brothers, sister, mother and father all in wolf form. He sent for Jacob and his brother immediately answered his call. *"South corner I am not sure of the smell, some type of cat"* his brother told him telepathically.

Jordan took a moment to focus, and within seconds pin-pointed the intruders. He sent out to his family *"There are five of them in the south corner. No one attacks except under my orders."* He had to add the last bit because his father was there. "Romano's go," he said, and the members of his family sprinted forward.

"Come on," the little panther sister said to her brothers telepathically. *"Mom and Dad told us to wait, not break into someone's house."*

"Stop whining," the oldest brother replied. *"There is no one in there and I am not waiting out here."* The youngest brother gave the door a push, but the door didn't budge. He did it again and

the door just rattled.

"*Move, let me do it,*" the oldest brother said. He backed up slightly and then went charging at the door. He hit it with so much force it shattered into pieces.

"*Guys,*" the little sister whined again. "*We are in so much trouble.*"

"*Shut up and come on,*" the youngest brother said. The sister spotted a big tree that looked like she could hide next to it. She ran overand ducked behind itshivering from fear. She thought about shifting back into human but then she couldn't hear her mom and dad. She just sat there singing her favorite song, waiting.

Jordan called the family to a halt. He took a second to focus. There were three distinct smells to the right and two to the left. "*Mom, John, head right. I sense three in that direction. My brothers and I will go left. Amara, I want you to cover the perimeter in case we have a runner or an unexpected visitor.*"

Diane and John approached the renter's house from the rear. They crept soundlessly . Diane saw movement from inside the house and told her husband to look in the same direction. John spotted the movement too, but couldn't make out anything. The two of them fell in sync, creeping towards the house silently. They used their decades of being together to predict and mimic each other's moves.

The couple circled the house,trying to find how the intruders entered. They noticed the front door was shattered. As they entered, the pair heard sounds coming from the kitchen. They crept through the house silently, the only thing giving them away was their smell.

In the kitchen the brothers had shifted to humans. "Do you smell that?" the youngest brother said, sniffing the air.

"Someone else is here."

"It's probably our sister coming in," the oldest brother turned his attention back towards the refrigerator. "There's not any food in here, just little chunks of cheese and bottled water. What type of house is this?"

The youngest brother knew their sense of smell was stronger in animal form than in human form, but he also knew that smell wasn't his sisters. He shifted back to his panther form, took a deep breath, and scanned his surroundings. As soon as he faced the entryway to the kitchen, he let out a mix between a growl and a yelp. The sound startled the oldest brother who slammed the refrigerator door and turned around. The youngest brother, who was technically still a cub, was trembling at the sight of the two large wolves. He glanced quickly at his brother who looked back at him looking just as scared as he was.

Diane looked at the two of them and said, "They're just kids John." The youngest one was in panther form so she could communicate with him. "Are you boys lost?" she asked, sitting on her hind legs to make herself seem less threatening. Beside her John was still at attention. She turned and growled at him. He looked at her and hesitantly sat on his hind legs. Diane turned her attention back to the boy. *"What are you guys doing here?"* she tried again telepathically.

The two brothers were terrified. *"Mom, help,"* The youngest one called out to their mother. The mother immediately called back, *"Run."*

"We will not let them get away," John said when they heard the order and then advanced on the two young panthers.

The oldest panther was so scared his reflexes forced a shift. In seconds he was a panther, just like his brother, and John took that as a challenge.

"John no," Diane cried, but it was too late. John lunged at the oldest brother. Panicking, the boy swiped out his paw and caught John across his cheek, with four incisions going from his ear to his mouth. He growled and jumped on the oldest brother. John pinned him to the ground and growled viciously at him.

The boy closed his eyes, knowing John was about to deliver a deadly blow. The youngest brother stood there not knowing what to do. *"Mom,"* he called out again. "There are wolves here, one of them is about to kill Ronny."

Diane finally understood that the boys had not been taught how to communicate between species yet. He was speaking to his mother not knowing her, her children, and John could understand what they were saying. Diane decided she would call out to the mother letting her know her children were in no harm, then she would deal with John. Before she could finish the thought, she heard a deafening roar.

The Romano brothers heard the child call to his mother and decided to remain still. The mother would not leave her children, knowing they might be in danger. The wolves had been tracking the cats around in circles. It frustrated Jordan that they were always a step behind them. Jordan called out to his mother asking her if she heard the child. His mother said that they were in the rental property with two panther cubs and they were terrified.

Jordan sighed heavily. *"Mother, don't let the fact that they are children hinder your judgment. These panthers would not have brought their children here if they weren't a benefit to them."*

His mother did not respond, but he knew she heard him. She had done that before, let her big heart and mothering instincts hinder her judgement.

Jacob fell back a few hundred yards to watch his brother's

back. Jordan and Jonathan were about a hundred yards apart walking using their enhanced senses. Suddenly, they heard a child call out *'Mom.'* Jordan called out to his brothers, "*Our mother says they are panthers. She and John have two cubs who just called the mother for help. We will split up and head towards the rental property, Ambush them there.*"

Right before the brothers broke up, they heard the child say his brother was in danger and the female panther let out a ferocious roar. Jordan grumbled and wondered what John had done. The brothers took off in the direction of the house.

"*John see, look what you've done,*" Diane scolded.

"*They came to our property looking for a fight Diane, there is no other reason for them to be there other than to challenge Jordan.*"

"*Let the boy go,*" Diane snapped. "*He is just a cub.*"

"*Don't start that just a cub stuff.*"

Diane was furious. Both her husband and her son did not have faith that she could navigate this situation with a level head. Before she could respond Jordan yelled, "*Attack.*" Diane looked at the little brother in front of her shivering in fear. She had no time and no other choice.

She growled at the little boy and advanced on him, causing him to back up with every step she took. She grabbed him by the neck, pulling him into the dining room. John was struggling to try to bring the oldest brother, who wouldn't stay still. Diane winced as she watched her husband bite down hard on the boy's neck to get him to stop moving around. The boy, but stopped.

There was a crash behind them and the couple, spun around with their snout close to the ground, and backs arched. Through the glass leapt two large panthers, who landed with a roar. The mother was calling out to her children.

Diane spoke to the mother. "*It is very dangerous of you to not teach your children how to communicate across species. Here they are, caught intruding on Romano property, and they can't communicate with me because they have not been taught."*

"I will fight for my children," The panther mother said. Just then the other panther lunged at Diane.. John jumped in front of her to protect her. .

John lunged as the panther was flying across the air. The two collided in the air and John stuck, both paws deep in the panther's neck. The panther clawed at John's shoulders, ripping and scratching. The two animals hit the ground, with John on top pinning the panther to the ground with his paws still embedded in the panther's neck.

Mother Panther ignored her husband and crept towards her two children, when glass broke behind her. Spinning around, there were three wolves behind her and the wolf standing between her and her children.

Jordan and his brothers entered the kitchen. Jordan pushed his Alpha power through the room. "Now I give you the chance to bow to your Alpha," he called out. His brothers bowed behind him. His mother bowed before her son graciously. John hesitantly released the panther who whimpered and bowed slightly to his son. The panther on the floor rose to his feet, despite his wounds.

"I will not say again," Jordan repeated. The mother panther reluctantly bowed before the North American Alpha, but the father panther refused.

"No wolf is my Alpha," he called out.

Amara, coming from the front of the house dragging a smaller cub in her teeth, called out, *"Here I come brother, to show my respect to my Alpha."* She bowed before Jordan without releasing the cub.

The mother seeing her daughter began to beg, *"Jordan Romano, Alpha of the Romano pack and Leader of the North American packs please forgive my family and release us without harm."*

"Too late for formalities intruder. My land and my family have been disrespected by this family and pack rules have been broken. This family will be punished," Jordan walked over to the father panther and embedded his nails into the back of the panther's neck. Jordan pressed his nose into the floor. *"When I say bow before me, I mean bow before me. Only two Alphas get the respect of a bow from any pack. Their pack Alpha. And me."*

Blood oozed around the neck of the panther. His wife buried her nose under her paws and whimpered, pleading with Jordan for mercy.

Jordan continued, *"Mother, Amara, take these children to the shed of this house."* Jordan looked at the mother panther. *"Since you put your cubs in danger by bringing them here and not teaching them how to communicate across species you will tell your children to follow Diane and Amara without hesitancy."*

The mother panther quickly called out to her children letting her know to go with the two wolves. Jordan released the male panther, flung him across the room towards his wife. Jordan needed that show of power for the panther to fall in line and start respecting him. The mother panther shifted back into human. "We have a bag in our car by the road. Please allow us to dress."

#

Jordan called out to his brothers only and told them he would return quickly and left the house. Sprinting through the woods, he went back towards the houses. Grabbing items from his family's bags in the front closets, he puts everything into one duffle bag. In his house, Jordan puts on sweatpants and a t-shirt and searches for his phone. He called Jelena.

Jelena: So, now I get an 'I'm sorry I hung up on -

Jordan: I need a favor and I will explain later.

Jelena: What's wrong?

Jordan: Do you have medics or doctors that help shifters when you come across them?

Jelena: Yes, we do, Jordan. What is going on?

Jordan: Come to the rental place with that doctor. No one else, the problem I have will be dealt with through the pack. Okay?

Jelena: On the way.

Jordan placed his phone in his pocket and headed back to the rental house. He drove because running on two feet was much slower than on four. He returned and allowed everyone to shift and put on clothes.

"What do you want us to do with them?" Amara asked Jordan.

"Question them," Jordan said matter-of-factly.

"Jordan, do not forget they are just kids." Diane said firmly.

"We need to figure out who they are and what they are doing here. They will be going up against the council, the whole family," Jordan said.

"Jordan," Diane began.

"Mother," Jordan interrupted. "The whole family partici-pated; the whole family will be punished. Either the council can punish them, or I will," Jordan commanded.

Diane walked over to the panther cubs and held up the clothes. She hoped they got the message.

Jordan looked at Amara. "Don't let her judgement get in the way."

Amara turned towards her mother and the cubs. Jordan picked up the two duffle bags and headed to the main house.

Once Jelena got to the house, she pulled up the driveway instead of parking on the street. Following her was a blue car with Dr. Rolands inside. Dr. Rolands was the doctor that the SID used when they had wounded individuals who couldn't go to the hospital.

Jelena hopped out of her car with Dr. Rolands doing the same and headed to the door. Jelena gasped at the damage to the front door, relieved that she decided to gear up under her sweat suit. The two women climbed through the broken door and paused.

Jelena did not think it was smart to go walking through a dark house where there were wolves and God knows what other animals wandering around. She turned around towards Dr. Rolands. "We should wait." Dr. Rolands agreed.

"What are you doing waiting here?" Jordan asked when he approached them.

Jelena shrugged. "I thought it would be a good idea to wait here instead of roaming through the jungle."

"Come this way," Jordan chuckled and Jelena exhaled. Jordan noticed for the first time that Jelena was not by herself.

He stuck his hand out when Dr. Rolands bowed. "Mr. Romano, nice to meet you."

"Handshakes and Jordan are fine Dr. -" Jordan chuckled again

"I am Dr. Rolands." Dr. Rolands face turned beet red

"All humans back here, I promise," he said.

They followed him through the house to the kitchen area. Jelena looked at the broken windows and glass everywhere "I guess I won't be moving in tomorrow," she muttered.

"Yes, you will," Jordan said glancing back. "It will be fixed by the time you get here."

"I still have to buy furniture and," she paused, embarrassed.

"Well everything, I have to buy everything."

"Don't worry," Jordan said nonchalantly "I am leaving the staging for you to keep."

Jelena's mouth dropped open. Before she had a chance to speak Jordan said, "Mother, Father this is Jelena Cohert and Dr. Rolands. Dr. Rolands is here to attend to the intruder."

Jelena's brow furrowed. "Intruders. You missed some details over the phone."

Jordan stared at her, the unfamiliar feeling in his gut rising, as the doctor hurried to tend to the man with gaping wounds on his neck. He was attuned only to Jelena, the vanilla smell; the break in her smooth skin in between her eyebrows indicating her displeasure with him. Her heartbeat was going slightly faster than normal, indicating she was off balance. He wished he could touch and taste her to satisfy his remaining senses.

Jelena held her hand up, palm facing Jordan. "Okay, right now you look like you want to eat me," she whispered, crossing her arms "So cut that out and get to explaining."

Jordan's eyebrow and he heard light footsteps approaching, stopping him from responding. Diane appeared and placed a hand on her son's shoulder. "I get it now."

She chuckled.

"You get what?

Diane just turned towards Jelena and stuck her hand out. Reluctantly Jelena took her hand and Diane placed her other hand on top of Jelena's. "It seems like we are both missing information here dear," Diane said. "Come this way and we will chat while the doctor is working."

Diane let go of Jelena's hands and placed her hand on the back of her shoulder to guide her. Jelena looked back and gave Jordan a 'help me' look. Jordan shrugged and turned towards the doctor.

Diane walked Jelena over to where the windows were broken. As they crunched the glass beneath their feet Diane winced. "I am sorry dear; our guy is on his way to clean all this up as we speak."

Jelena nodded, unsure how to respond. The last time she saw her Jelena detected hostility.

Diane turned and looked at Jelena. "Tell me what you do?"

"I am a Senior Agent with the FBI," she replied hesitantly.

"In what capacity do you work with my son?"

"I am a part of a special division that investigates shifter crimes."

"So you hunt my kind?" she asked suspiciously.

"I hunt those who commit murder," Jelena said. "Whether they are human or shifter."

Diane smirked, "I see why my son is smitten with you."

"He looks like he wants to eat me, but that's about it," Jelena chuckled nervously.

Diane shook her head. "In due time my dear, in due time." She proceeded to tell Jelena all that had happened with the panthers. After their discussion, they walked back over and joined Jordan, John and Dr. Rolands working on the panther. His wife sat next to him, sobbing. Jelena felt sorry for them.

Jelena punched Jordan in the arm. "You were on the phone with me before everything went to hell and couldn't give me a heads up?"

"I didn't know what was going on," Jordan said, rubbing his arm.

"I don't turn into any animal, but I have been doing this for almost 20 years and I know a few things. I already told you –"

Jordan cut her off. "I'm sorry," he apologized. "I was scared and wasn't thinking."

His words made her deflate. "So where are we now?" Jelena asked.

"The kids say they were just supposed to sit and wait in the car," Diane said. "The boys became restless and got out to wander when they came upon the house."

"That is the truth," the Mother said. "There is a guy in town, Andre, he is a friend of the family."

"A hyena from Africa?"Jordan asked

"Yes," the Mother blurted out, sobbing. "He said he needed us to go on the Romano property, sneak up to the main house, and break in. We were just supposed to make a mess of the place."

"Our family, my father, is in debt to his father. We have secrets that can't be exposed, we had no choice. Please have mercy on us."

Jordan's rage bubbled up from deep in his gut and pushed his Alpha power through the room. Jelena's senses perked up, confused about what had her on edge. She guessed it was Jordan by the way everyone took a step back and bowed their heads.

Jelena put her hand on Jordan's shoulder. "Stop flinging podér around, you are scaring them."

Jordan turned to look at her and instantly felt his rage disappear."You were nowhere near my house. Why start down here?" Jordan asked.

"We wanted to sneak up to see if anyone was home. We did not want to do this Alpha Romano –"

"Call him Jordan," Jelena broke in.

The corners of Jordan's mouth turned up and he jutted his chin towards the panther, giving her permission.

"J – Jordan, we had no choice, we are in debt to the hyenas."

"What debt does your father owe to the hyenas?" Jordan inquired.

"I don't know the details. All I know is that we had no choice. My children have nothing to do with this, we couldn't just leave them."

"So, what happens now?" Jelena asked.

"We will see about the injuries and I will notify the council. Once his injuries are tended to, they will be released."

Jelena did not think it was a good idea to send them to the council but would not question him. She stood straighter. Dr. Rolands came out. The doctor explained the panther was okay and needed to rest for a few hours and he would heal completely, thanks to his accelerated healing powers. Dr. Rolands wiped her hands on a towel, "Thankfully, no organs or arteries were damaged."

Jelena waited while Jordan handled what was going on. She was sure he didn't want her to just leave, and she needed to ask him about the house.

A few hours later, the panthers were reunited with their children. Once they left the property, Jordan's father was walking out of the house when Jordan called him back. The man scowled when Jordan called his name.

The family talked for a few more minutes and then they dispersed. Diane walked over to Jordan and hugged; and to Jelena's amazement she hugged her too.

Once alone in the house Jelena felt her muscles relax. "Looks like I won't be moving in anytime soon," she joked.

"No, you will, I will give you the keys the day after tomorrow at two o'clock, three at the latest."

#

"Why are you giving me all this furniture?" Jelena asked.

Jordan walked up to her so that their breath mingled in the same space. "Do you need the furniture?" he countered.

Jelena looked up at him, breathless. Her chin tilted back, lost in his chocolate brown eyes. Her breath caught, and she opened her mouth to speak but forgot the question he asked. As if reading her mind, he asked again, "Jelena, do you need the furniture?"

"You act like you know what's going on in my life." Jelena scowled., "how much has your brother told you?"

"You no longer live with your husband, that's all I know. The rest is inference."

"What have you inferred?" Jelena asked.

Jordan leaned into her, their lips centimeters apart. He heard her breath quickening, and her cheeks flushed with desire. When he spoke, his lips brushed hers. "There is a reason why you still wear your wedding ring, but are looking for a place to live by yourself."

Jelena's mind was telling her to take a step back but her body refused to move. Breathless, she said, "I got kidnapped and tortured and my husband got controlling and abusive. I already had one abusive husband, I don't care to deal with a second one."

Rage built up inside Jordan. "Someone hit you?" he asked, his eyes glistening with gold, a sign the wolf was near.

Jelena felt a mixture of fear and admiration. "I was not abused; my spouses were abusive. I was a fighter," She stated flatly.

As if reading her mind, he said, "Fighting back still means you were abused."

"Well, he was abused too then," she replied matter-of-factly. His eyebrows raised in amusement. "What is so amusing about that?" she asked.

Jordan inhaled and exhaled slowly. Reminding Jelena how close they were to each other, her stomach twisted. "You are not a victim; I am sorry for implying that," he said in a low voice.

Jelena raised her chin in triumph. She immediately regretted the motion because it closed the small gap between their lips, and she kissed him.

She was about to pull back, but that millisecond is all Jordan needed to take control of her mouth. He placed his hands on either side of her face, so she couldn't back up and devoured her mouth. Caught in the passion and hunger, she stood on her tiptoes and in one fluid movement Jordan dropped his hands to her hips and lifted her up.

She wrapped her legs around his waist as he let go of her hips, grabbed a handful of her hair with one hand and the other grabbed the back of her shirt, shredding it to pieces. Lost in the moment, her hands quickly explored his body. He realized she had on the vest underneath and grinned.

"You ripped my shirt," Jelena managed to whisper before her mouth was devoured again. Jordan undid the vest and flung it. Jelena pulled at the bottom of his shirt, trying to lift it between them so she would get it off. Jordan released her hair, grabbed his shirt and pulled it, shredding it to pieces.

Jordan felt his phone vibrate in his pocket and ignored it. Then he heard a faint voice, his mother's voice, and he pulled back. Jelena stared at him, panting. "What?" she asked.

"My mother is calling," he groaned as he put her back on the ground.

Jelena put her hands on her hips and glared at him. Jordan shrugged. "Call me when you get home?" he said.

"Get home, with no shirt?" she rolled her eyes.

"I like this view," Jordan smirked. "Plus, the vest has good coverage too."

"I have a shirt in my car but that is beside the point," she huffed as she padded her pockets making sure she had her phone and keys. She grabbed the vest then turned to leave.

Chapter Thirteen

Move in and get Cozy

Jelena sat on the couch in Angela's apartment with her phone to her ear. She had just finished telling Angela that Diane had already called her letting her know the damage was fixed and she was ready to move in. She explained that Jordan gave her the furniture and how it was a relief she didn't need to spend money.

Angela went on and on about how she needed to meet Jordan because he is being too generous to be strictly professional. They chatted for a while and then Jelena told Angela she was getting the last of her things and to stop by her new place when she finished for the day. Hanging up, Jelena grabbed her duffle bags. She swung them over her shoulder and headed out of Angela's apartment for the last time.

Jelena was at her new place, in the master bedroom, setting everything up nice and neat, still amazed with the beauty of this house.

Inside the enormous master closet,oblivious to anything else, she felt breath on her neck. Her instinct kicked in and she jerked her head back, head butting the person behind her.

She heard a grunt and spun around, intending to punch the person behind her, but her hand was caught mid-air. Panting, she panicked and then relaxed the next moment when she heard a familiar voice say "Ouch."

Jelena relaxed. "Damn it Jordan," she scowled. "You scared this shit out of me."

"That actually hurt," he said, rubbing his nose, amazed that she had that much power.

"You cannot just walk in here whenever you please," she huffed, crossing her arms.

"We are supposed to meet today to go over the hyena's victims," he said, pouting with mock innocence.

"First of all we don't know if it was whatever hyena keeps being mentioned. Do not make assumptions until all the evidence is in. Second off you cannot break into here!or use any key you may have," she added quickly. Jordan did not respond immediately, and Jelena raised her eyebrow.

"Okay, okay,"Jordan smirked and raised his hands in a surrender motion."I will only come in when invited. Even though that's against my nature."

"Vampire joke huh," Jelena smirked.

Jordan clasps his hands together. "So," he said slowly and then faded away. Jelena waited for him to finish his sentence. When he didn't, she turned around and looked at him. He was ringing his hands together, his eyes jerking around the room.

"Why Mr. Romano," she cooed. "Are you nervous about something?"

Jelena's voice jerked Jordan from the thoughts in his head. "What? I am not nervous about anything."

Jelena rolled her eyes and walked past him to exit the closet. He did not move to the side making their bodies touch. He inhaled sharply, greedily taking in her scent. Jelena had to force herself not to stop and jump him right then and there.

In the bedroom, Jelena made herself busy, not sure exactly what to do next. She couldn't believe she was nervous. Her phone chirped, and she was grateful for the distraction.

"Do you mind going down and opening the door? My friend Angela is here."

Jordan left the room. Jelena rotated her neck and moved her arms back and forth, releasing the tension she didn't even know she was holding. She sat down on her bed trying to figure out this feeling. *Cálmate*, she told herself. She was feeling giddy, and it bugged her. She was an adult acting like a teenager. *That's it*, she thought. *I have butterflies.*

Downstairs Jordan opened the door and smiled politely.

Angela went in for a hug but stopped short. "Who are you?" she asked.

Jordan leaned against the doorframe. "Well it seems like I am owed the explanation due to you being on that side of the door."

Angela crossed her arms. "This is Jelena's house. So, I ask again, who are you?"

Jordan chuckled. "I can see why you two are friends." He stuck his hand out. "I am Jordan, and you must be Angela?"

"Ohh, so you're Jordan" she grinned. "Yes, I am Angela, Angela Rodriguez."

Jordan motioned for her to come in. "This is beautiful" she said as she walked though, taking everything in. Jelena came down the stairs.

"Hola chica," <hey girl> Jelena said, animatedly.

"Esto es hermoso, mi gusta mucho," Angela said and added with a wink. "El hombre es atractivo. <This is beautiful, I like it very much. The Man is attractive>

Jordan looked at the two wide-eyed. "Hold up, I am just learning, you to have to do Spanish 101 for me."

Jelena laughed. "Not everything is meant for you to understand. Think of it as our own form of telepathy." Jelena turned towards Angela., "I haven't been shopping today but do you want a drink?"

"I'll go get something," Angela replied.

Slightly disappointed she didn't have a reason to get away from Jordan, Jelena stood there awkwardly. "Where are all the boxes?" he said, cutting through the tension.

Jelena's forehead wrinkled. "What boxes?"

Jordan walked over to the living room and casually sat down. "Ya' know, aren't cops supposed to carry their files and stuff in boxes?"

Jelena chuckled and walked into the living room, sitting on the other side of the room. "Some of our files are paper," she said reaching over and handing him one of the tablets that was on the table. "But most of them are electronic."

"Fancy," he smirked, turning on the tablet and swiping through the screen. Jelena hid her grin and looked down at her hands.

Angela walked in. "¿Qué te pasa, porque te sientas alli?" <What's wrong with you, sitting over there>

Jelena looked up at her and cocked her head.. Angela came and sat in an open space "So, what do you guys got so far?"

Thankful for a subject change Jelena responded, "We are waiting on Michaels, then I will go over with the guys what is in the system so far."

Jordan, who was stuck in a trance looking at Jelena, said, "Oh we are just waiting for my brother? I will go get him."

"No, it's okay. I told him what time to come. He is actually going to be there at that time, not an hour beforehand." Jelena stared at him, waiting for him to say something fliplant to her remark, but Jordan was paying her no attention.

I want him to be looking at me, she thought.

Jordan put his phone down. "He is on his way. You know we all live on this property, right? The Alpha's immediate family has to live on the same property as him."

Angela's brow crinkled in confusion. "Alpha? You mean like Jacob from Twilight?"

"I may not have told you everything Ang," Jelena said, guilty.

Angela's eyes got wide, and she looked from Jordan to Jelena. "You mean actually like Jacob?"

"Wait, my brother did what?"Jordan asked, confused.

"Jacob is your brother!" Angela squealed.

Jelena held up her hands. "Hold on," she looked at Angela. "I am pretty sure he isn't related to a fictional character."

"Fictional character?" Jordan said, getting even more con-fused.

"She means Jacob Black, from Twilight," Jelena explained. "I didn't even know you had more than one brother."

"Oh," Jordan said catching on. "Yea, I have two brothers and a sister. You never told her I was a shifter?"

Angela nearly jumped out of her chair. "Show me," she squealed.

"Um, I don't think that is a good idea," Jelena said cautiously.

Jordan shrugged his shoulders, "I'm down if you are."

Angela jumped up and clapped her hands and then she clasped them together and sat back in the chair. She took a deep breath. "I would love you to."

Jordan began to undress, and Jelena was about to protest. Not because she had an issue with Angela seeing Jordan in wolf form. She had an issue with Angela seeing Jordan naked. Before she could say anything, her phone rang. Jelena felt around her pockets for her phone and pulled it out, groaning when she saw the caller ID.

Jordan was unbuckling his pants when he heard Jelena's phone ring. He was amused by Angela sitting on the couch like a kid in a candy store waiting for him to shift, that he ignored it at first. What caught his attention was her groan, her heartbeat quickening. It was someone she didn't want to talk to. He paused and watched her answer the call and walk out of earshot of Angela.

His ears twitched as he listened to both sides of the conversation. He didn't notice Angela's confusion. He heard Jelena having a heated conversation with a guy who was upset because she wasn't answering the door. They argued back and forth about Jelena moving and she was not telling him where. *Maybe her still married ex-husband* he thought.

"Never mind, I guess," Angela shouted annoyed.. She had been calling his name, and he was completely ignoring her. She couldn't believe he was so into Jelena that when she stepped away, he was rude to her. She jumped when his head snapped around and he asked her "What is Jelena's husband's name?"

That caught her off guard. "Do you have super hearing or something?" she asked him.

"Yes, I do. I'm sure Jelena will tell you all about my abilities later, can I have his name now please?" he grumbled. He wanted to know what her husband's name was because he was pretty sure she wouldn't tell him.

Sensing an urgency in his tone, Angela told him. Just then, there was a knock at the door. Angela went to answer it and Jordan went back to listening to Jelena's conversation.

At the door Angela greeted Michaels. They entered the house chatting with each other. Michaels said, "Hey bro," but stopped when Jordan didn't respond. Michaels focused on his own enhanced hearing, fearing another intruder. He quickly realized Jordan was just eavesdropping and followed Angela to the living room.

"So, you must be Sam," she said.

"Nope, I am more like Seth," he responded.

Angela playfully punched him in the arm. "You get the reference, two points for you."

"I have daughters," he explained.

Jelena entered the room and felt Jordan's stare. He didn't look as if he wanted to eat her, as usual. This look said something else that she couldn't put her finger on, el la estaba confundiendo a ella. <he was confusing her> Using Michaels as a distraction she went over and greeted him.

"Ang is on the team?" he asked Jelena.

"No, she was supposed to be here in a strictly friend capacity when Jordan showed up seven hours ahead of time and told her he turns into animals."

"Did Jordan have a Twilight reference too?" Michaels chuckled.

"I have no idea what a Twilight is." Jordan said, rolling his eyes while the rest of the room broke into laughter.

"You need to have a movie night with your nieces bro," Michaels said.

"Pop culture lesson later," Jelena jumped in. "Let's get down to business."

We got a serial

"Our first female victim is Jane Hawthorne, 25. She was found in the back of her dorm building. She had four bite marks on her neck." Cohert was going through the files telling everyone what they had on the seven victims.

"Second female is Magrette Mathews, 22. She was found in an alley with slash marks and deep incisions all over her body. Her carotid artery was punctured, she bled out instantly. There is no reference to what made the marks."

Rodriguez was looking over Cohert's shoulder as she swiped through the files. "Okay, the first picture looked like she was bitten by some animal. It was four puncture holes right at the carotid artery. Why the hell did he switch from that to slashing her all up like this? Are there any interview transcripts in the files?" She was wondering what the victim was doing before she got killed.

"Maybe he intended to kill her the same way, but she fought back or made him mad. Or maybe he is trying to change up what he does to throw the police off," she said, thinking aloud.

"I don't think he was thinking that thoroughly, to change up his MO," Michaels said. "According to him, he wanted to get our attention or the attention of our father. So, he is probably just escalating to catch our attention."

"I know you guys have a suspect in mind," Cohert began, "but we can't let that color our judgment." Cohert looked at Jordan to see if he had any input. When he didn't say anything, she continued. "Danielle Toppson, 25. She was found in her room by her roommate with slash marks all over her neck and upper body. The wounds were so deep one of her arms was hanging on by a tendon."

Cohert went through descriptions of the final four victims: Michelle Clemonds 23, Frances Stevens 21, Tonya Ellps 18 and Lisa Hemmingway 16. All seven victims were under the age of 25. The last four were found in wooded areas within a 15-mile radius. "All seven victims were killed exactly 30 days apart. The only victim with bite marks was the first victim. The rest had slash marks or a combination of both."

Cohert sat her tablet on her lap and looked around the room.

"There are no interviews in these files," Rodriguez started to say." It's like no one followed up on the deaths."

"This guy was a full-blown serial killer months ago and no one investigated," Michaels continued with an irritated tone.

"Esperate,"<wait> Rodriguez said. "Bite marks and slashes, were these all done by shape shifters?"

Jelena looked at her friend guiltily. "There is a lot I have to fill you in on Rodriguez. We haven't had a lot of time since your promotion. I wasn't expecting you to be here at the same time as the guys," Jelena gave Jordan a pointed look. When he didn't say anything, she continued. "I am a part of the special investigation division."

Rodriguez ran her fingers through her hair. "And I gather that the special cases that division gets cand are not allowed to tell anyone about have to do with shape shifters?"

"Just shifters Rodriguez," Jordan said, catching on with the switch from first names to last names.

Rodriguez looked at him apologetically, "Sorry, I am new at this.".

"You are taking it well though" Jordan commented, sitting stoically in his chair.

"Rodriguez," Cohert said. "Your promotion elevated your security clearance. Every Senior Agent and above knows what the SID does, it is just kept secret."

"It's the job," Rodriguez said, waving her hands from side to side. "No, I get it. So, a shifter has been killing one girl a month, and no one has been investigating until they gave it to you guys?"

"Usually the corner looks for indicators and then lets the Chief of Police know that a case in 'non investigable' this tells them that it gets bumped to the SID. I do not know what happened with the earlier cases, but Stevens and Hemmingway were held because of Highworth and then Kinkcade."

"That big scandal with the medical examiner's office," Michaels spoke up. "Ya' haven't heard of that? A new ME was hired. The old was forced to resign."

"Okay so the ball was dropped during the switch," Rodriguez said slowly, still processing all the new information. "What is our next move?"

"Your next move is to continue to lead the Kinkcade investigation with Belle and Jonathan will continue working the Highworth investigation with Spearman and Bell without the e.. Michaels and I are being pulled for this investigation. We do not have a third person on our team right now, so Jordan is a consultant filling in."

Rodriguez got really animated, her thick Spanish accent becoming more pronounced "So you are just going to drop this on me and tell me go back and look for Kinkcade?" she said.

Cohert gave her a look of surprise and Rodriguez put her hands up in a surrender motion "Not that Kinkcade isn't important to find," she said back tracking.

Cohert turned towards Michaels feeling a little hurt at Rodriguez' statement. "We will split the list and do interviews of the victim's family and friends. I think that is a good place to start."

Cohert then turned to Jordan who was sitting there quietly. "If you could check into the Andre person and get some information on that. I can get someone to run him down and do some surveillance."

"Broke in here," Rodriguez shrieked. "While you were in here?"

"I would never let any harm come of Cohert," He defended, letting her last name roll around his tongue. He disliked saying her husband's last name. But he had already caught on to the name changes when they began to talk about the cases.

"Whoa," Rodriguez mumbled. "That was kinda' scary." Then she turned to Cohert. "Listen girl, I really didn't mean to sound like Kinkcade isn't important. Of course, the guy who tortured and tried to kill my best friend needs to be found, lo siento. I have a date tonight and surveillance after that with Belle. We have Zumba this week, right?"

"Yeah," Cohert sighed. "See you then."

Jordan felt his phone buzz in his pocket and stepped out to take the call.

"I will take Mathews, Toppson, Clemonds, and Hawthorne which leaves you with Stevens, Ellps and Hemmingway; that cool?" Michaels asked.

"Yeah, that's fine. Interview them and anyone else that pops up in their statements. I will do the same as well as run the theory with Jordan. Can you also get any evidence reports from your four victims and go over those, follow up on anything that needs to be followed up on and run anything that hasn't been run?"

\#

"Gotcha," Michaels replied. He stood up to leave and hesitated slightly.

"Michaels I am doing fine, I promise" she said trying to reassure him. She lifted her arms up and rotated side to side, showing him her range of motion.

"It's not that," he said. "I see you are still wearing your wedding ring. What is going on there?"

The question caught her off guard. Jelena's head tilted to one side as she thought about where this conversation was headed. She decided to be honest with him. He has been her partner before and is her partner now. She knew his big secret, and it was time to leave her cards on the table. "My husband and I are separated, not legally though. He became–uhh–we had some issues after I got back from the hospital," she said. She averted her eye contact at the last minute and Michaels jumped on her attempt to withhold information.

"He hit you," Michaels asked forcefully, sparkled with red. She knew that when a shifter's eyes turned colors, it was a sign the animal was near.

"Michaels," she cooed softly. "It is okay. I still have on my wedding ring because, um, well, I am not sure why I still wear it," she said as her shoulders deflated, and she averted her eyes. She blinked rapidly to hold back the tears.

"Well, you can take that shit off because you will not be going back to him," Michaels was pacing back and forth. "Does Jordan know his man has been hitting you? That same guy who I met. I am going to tell Jordan; we will handle him."

All the strength she had that was keeping the tears at bay melted away and they began to flow. Her brother and father did not act this way when she told them about Alejandro, which kept her from being completely honest about Dan. She felt a swell of emotion that was unfamiliar to her bubble up. "Don't hurt him, let me handle it, please?" she pleaded.

Michaels stopped pacing at the sound of her broken voice, looked at her and he softened. "I'm sorry," he said, stretching his arms out, inviting her in for a hug.

Jelena melted in his arms and began sobbing.

She was frustrated with another failed marriage. She was frustrated that she had to start over. She was frustrated that Kinkcade kidnapped her. She was frustrated that Dan was trying so hard to control her. She was frustrated with what her life had become in two short months and she was sick and tired of keeping all those emotions in.

Michaels had embraced her and the comfort she was receiving from him and the passion in his eyes was something she had never experienced before. She didn't know how to deal with it and she didn't know how to react.

Jordan walked back in the room and barked, "What happened?" making Jelena jump.

Michaels looked at his brother and growled, "Did you know her husband was beating her?"

Jelena popped her head up, "He was not beating me." Jordan cut her off, "Yeah, she told me, something new happened?"

"Are we going to do something about it?" Michaels asked his brother.

"No! I am handling it." she said.

Jordan looked at his brother and raised his eyebrow. Michaels got the message and let go of Jelena

"Got it," he said more to Jordan than to Jelena. "Alright, I will talk to y'all later."

Jelena looked at Jordan, "I'm sorry, I'm not sure what came over me." She chuckled, embarrassed that she broke down like that in front of them. Especially Jordan. "That was embarrassing, I didn't mean to break down like that."

"Looked like you needed to, like you were holding back a lot of emotions," He said apprehensively. He wanted her to open up to him but didn't want to push her.

Jelena took a deep breath and wiped her face. "I don't know why but I seem to trust you. I know better than to trust someone I just met, but I can't explain it."

"Don't fight it," he told her.

Jelena sighed heavily, and against her better judgment decided to open up to him.

Jelena and Jordan sat on the couches and told him everything from Alejandro, to how her father and brother reacted to her, what she thought, great relationship with Dan. When she finally stopped and looked at him, she saw the gold in his eyes. The color flickered back and forth like he was fighting to keep the wolf away.

"Please say something," she pleaded.

Jordan took a few deep breaths to calm himself. When he finally spoke, his voice was low and raspy. "I know you don't like being called a victim but that is what you are. Or maybe we should say a survivor. Either way, I need you to accept help. I need you to accept my help."

"I don't want you to hurt him Jordan," Jelena said and then quickly added. "You or any Romano."

Jordan looked away. Jelena really didn't want Dan to be hurt, but she also felt something really strong connecting her to Jordan. She was sure she was going to give Dan enough time to relax and then work on her marriage. She had been married for almost 20 years and that was nothing to give up on. But sitting here, in this moment with Jordan trumped everything, even the muy caliente moment they had before.

Jelena slid over on the couch and leaned into Jordan, resting her head on the inside of his shoulder. Jordan welcomed this act of intimacy and inhaled deeply, greedily gulping up the vanilla scent he has come to depend on.

"I have to figure out what I am going to do," she said quietly.

Jordan rested his chin on Jelena's head and agreed to her unspoken request to let her handle it. He had no idea what drew him to her so quickly and intensely. What he did know was that her reconciling with her husband was not an option. She was his and he would do whatever it took to help her see that.

As Jelena rested on his shoulder, she wondered about the intense feelings she was having. She had no idea what drew her to him so quickly; she trusted him completely, and she knew better than that. She had no idea what was happening to her, but what she did know was that she no longer wanted to reconcile with Dan. She wanted Jordan and would take the steps to end her marriage so she could have him.

What are we, where do we see this going?

A ngela drove to the restaurant feeling guilty. She didn't mean for it to sound like she didn't want to find Kinkcade and wanted to be on the shifter case instead. What made her feel really guilty is that, that's actually how she felt. She knew Kinkcade was important and needed to be found. Especially for what he did to Jelena. But, how could she not get excited about shifters? She would much rather be hunting people who turned into animals than Kinkcade. She still felt bad that she made Jelena felt like she wasn't important though.

Angela pulled up to the restaurant and parked. She's heard of this place before and it was way fancier than what she was dressed for. She pulled out her phone and texted Cassidy:

Angela: I can't go in there; I have to go home and change.

Cassidy: You better not come in here now.

Angela sighed and hung her phone back on the attachment on her vent. She was wearing jeans and a tank top with a cute leather jacket.

This place was at least four stars, she knew that for a fact. She really didn't want to go in here and embarrass herself. On top of that, all the other women in their evening gowns and fancy clothes would be looking down on her and that would piss her off.

She thought of texting Cassidy again and telling him she was going to change.

He made a reservation though. *What would Jelena say?* She thought to herself. *"¡Basta! Just go ahead on the date. Forget what those snobby women think,"* she pictured Jelena saying.

So, she grabbed her phone and her clutch and got out of the car.

When Angela walked into the restaurant, she was in awe. The place looked even nicer than she assumed it would. She felt more self-conscious the farther in the building she got. She approached the hostess podium and was met by a smiling redhead.

"Hello, welcome to The Rich Table's casual night. My name is Bella, just one?"

Angela smirked, *Casual night* she thought. "I am here for the Firestone reservation," she replied.

Bella looked down at the list in front of her, "Aha, right this way ma'am."

As Angela followed Bella through the restaurant, she looked around at the tables. Everyone had on jeans and t-shirts, shorts and hoodies. Angela giggled that Cassidy would take her to a fancy restaurant on the one night everyone isn't dressed fancy.

As Bella approached the table, she looked over and saw Cassidy with a wide grin.

"Here you go," Bella said, handing her a menu. "Your waiter will be with you shortly."

Angela took the menu and sat down. She glanced at Cassidy before looking down at the menu.

"We are just going to overlook your overreaction huh?" he chuckled.

Angela looked up from the menu."Yes. I was in the car freaking out," she admitted..

"Since when do you get insecure?" he asked.

"No one said I am insecure; I just didn't want to be embarrassed," she countered.

"Embarrassment stems from insecurities. Even if this wasn't a casual night, you have nothing to be insecure about," he said looking her intently in the eyes.

His comments made her blush, and she hid this fact by looking back down at the menu. Once the waiter arrived, they ordered wine, and their entrees.

They were engrossed in a conversation about the similarities in the way they were raised being from different continents. Angela didn't know why she believed London didn't have any rough neighborhoods.

When the food arrived, they stopped talking. As the waiter was putting down their plates, Cassidy's phone buzzed on the table. Angela watched him check it and then put it back on the table but face down.

"¿Quien esta en el telefono?" <Who is on the phone> she asked.

"Huh?" he said confused.

"Who's on the phone?" she said in English.

"Oh," he said nonchalantly. "No one, I can answer it later."

"Fine," she said shortly and then started her dinner.

Firestone stared at her confused. They ate for the next few moments in silence. He couldn't take the silence anymore and asked, "What happened?"

"What do you mean what happened?" she responded, still engrossed in her food.

"Your mood changed," he replied. "Just be honest Ang."

Angela sighed heavily and put her fork down. "What are we, where do you see this going?"

A little caught off by the question he put his fork down and gave her his attention. "Well," he began.

"Because I need to know whether to be mad that you are hiding whoever is texting you. If I don't have a right to be mad, I need to know now so I can calm myself down," she said in one large breath.

"I didn't mean to upset you," he told her.

"Are we together?" she asked flatly, ignoring his apology.

"I would like us to be," he said. "We've never talked about it though."

"We have been acting like we are together, and maybe that is my fault for not setting boundaries in the beginning," she said swiftly. Without taking a breath she continued, "I don't get serious with someone often, but when I do, it is only one person at a time and I expect whoever I am dating to do the same."

"I do text other women and occasionally go on dates," Cassidy admitted.

"I don't want to be the only one spending energy on something that is not genuine," she explained, stung by the fact that he was dating other people .

"I did not know you wanted to be exclusive," he said.

"That wasn't an answer," she said blinking rapidly, trying to stop the tears from falling.

"I want to be with you," he said firmly.

"How can that be true when you're having sex with other people?" she growled..

"I want to be with you," he said again.

"What am I supposed to do with that?" she asked.

"That's where we move on from; me and you exclusively

together."

Angela shrugged and went back to her food. Cassidy continued staring at her, unsure why she still seemed upset.

The rest of the night the conversation seemed forced and not as easy as it had been. Angela and Cassidy said their goodbyes and went their separate ways.

On the way home to get ready to meet up with Belle, Angela called Jelena and told her about the conversation. Her friend assured her she got what she wanted in the end, becoming exclusive, and that she understood why but she could not be upset for him seeing other people when she didn't specify that that was something she wanted.

#

Jelena took a deep breath as she sat in her car outside of Dan's house. *It technically is still my house too*, she thought. She came over here to tell Dan she wanted to end it; she wanted a divorce. That was something she never thought she would say with Dan.

She swore they were going to work it out. That his behavior was due to the trauma he suffered when she was kidnapped. She couldn't fault him for his defense mechanisms and coping skills.

Then she met Jordan, and something was pulling her towards him. The feelings she felt for him intensified each day and she could no longer ignore it. It was unfair to Dan, limbo knowing Jordan was claiming her heart.

She took one more big breath and then got out of the car. She felt awkward knocking at this door; it was her door after all.

Dan opened the door with a grin. He stuck out his arms as if to hug her, "Jelena, your home."

Jelena stepped out of his grasp. "We have to talk Dan"

Emotion flashed in his eyes. It was gone so fast she couldn't identify it but she was sure it was the facade breaking.

He stepped back and ushered her in. As Jelena walked in the house, she looked around as if she never lived there. He had kept everything just as it was when she was there.

"Do you want a drink?" he asked.

"No, Dan," she replied, "we just need to talk. Can you come over here, please?" she asked, walking to the living room. Dan came to the entryway and leaned against the doorframe.

"Talk about what, Jelena?" he asked coldly flat, and void of any emotion.

Jelena felt a little nervous but slammed that down. She gave herself a pep talk remembering her grandmother and remembering the fact that she was a badass.

"I want a divorce," she said matter-of-factly. She stuck her hand in her pocket and touched her phone.

"No," he said.

"Dan, I am not asking you. I am letting you know I am going to file for divorce."

"What happened to work this out and counseling?" he spat out.

"I don't want that anymore," she said

"Since when?" he yelled.

"I have had time to think about my life and what I want to do with it."

"I don't care what you want to do with your life," he yelled. "It's another man, isn't it?" he looked at her with disgust. "You're fucking another man."

Jelena thought the best thing to do was to stay calm. "Dan I was in an abusive relationship before and that is not something I want to do again. I didn't want to throw away our 20 years, but this is a boundary I have to stay firm to."

Dan's head tilted to one side, and he stared at her for a moment blankly. Then a grin slowly stretched on his face. "I will never divorce you."

"Now I am pretty sure your brother and nosey friend knows you are here so you can leave now."

Dan walked over to the door and opened it, then looked back at Jelena. As she walked by him he whispered "*Never*" in her ear and then slammed the door behind her.

Party time

Party time

Jelena sat at the table in her dining room with a notebook, her laptop, her work tablet and pens sprayed about the table. Most of her day had been spent running around getting statements from the victims' families on her list. She had to type the statements so they could be formally entered into the system.

She had to go to the office to see what was in evidence and request the DNA from Hemmingway to be run. There were also hairs that were in evidence that had not been run yet. She picked up her notebook to look at the physical evidence list.

With a sigh, she slung the notebook back on the table. The DNA and hairs were the only evidence she had. What worried her is that if they were really dealing with a shifter, the DNA would come back inconclusive and the hairs would come back animal hairs. The case would be determined an accident, no matter how implausible it seemed.

She had many cases over the years get ruled an accident even though she knew there was a killer out there. If she was dealing with a human suspect, DNA and hair would be a slam dunk.

But a shifter would need to confess because physical evidence meant nothing when you have animal hair and DNA that no current technology can identify.

Her phone buzzed, and she jumped, thinking it was Jordan. She looked at the screen;it was a reminder for her to get ready for Zumba.

Jelena sighed with disappointment and then moved her head from side to side and rotated her shoulders. She had been sitting for too long and now Zumba would kick her ass.

Running late Jelena pulled up to Zumba and rushed inside. Jared, Chad and Angela were up front when she arrived. The first song was beginning, and she threw her stuff down and went to jump by her friends.

"Why are you late?" Angela asked.

"I was working," she panted/.

Angela raised one eyebrow and smirked.

"What?" she balked.

"Working on Jordan?" Angela giggled..

Jelena continued talking, ignoring Angela. "Okay, so this weekend his family is having their monthly family party thing, and he invited me–er–me, you and Cassidy," Jelena said while following the dance moves clumsily.

"He invited all of us, or did you invite all of us?" she asked.

"It is Saturday at 9, come to my house to get ready."

The instructor scowled at them through the mirror and they stopped talking and focused.

After the class, the group was drinking from their water bottles and chatting.

"Oh," Jelena said, "Jared make sure you give Angela a status update because we have a senior agent status update meeting with Monroe."

Angela looked at her surprised. "We do, since when?"

Jelena rolled her eyes "It's a new policy put in place by my father. All senior agents must do a weekly status meeting with their ASAC to try to prevent a Jackson situation from happening again."

Angela nodded. The room was starting to clear out, and the group gathered their belongings and headed towards the door.

"Speaking of Jackson," Jared said. "Do we know when we will have another SSA?"

Jelena didn't have to look to know everyone was staring at her waiting for her to answer.

"Guys, I do not have some straight line to the FBI behind the scenes. My father and I are not close, personally or professionally."

The group fell quiet until they exited the building. They said their goodbyes and the Bell brothers went one way and Angela and Jelena went the other.

"So, tell me about this party," Angela began.

The women arrived at Angela's car first. Jelena looked at Angela "All I know is that is casual wear and you and Cassidy are coming."

"Did he invite us, or did you invite us because you are scared of going by yourself?" Angela asked grinning.

Jelena rolled her eyes. "Listen, girl." she began. "I don't know what is going on between Jordan and I."

Angela wrinkled her eyebrows "Is that bad or good?"

"I just went to Dan, asked for a divorce," she said, avoiding eye contact. "He wouldn't go for it, of course, but until recently I didn't even want a divorce."

"What do you mean you didn't want a divorce," she said accusingly. Angela shook her head and said "wait no, one thing at a time.So, you have feelings for Jordan and because of this you asked Dan for a divorce?"

"Angela you don't understand," Jelena began. "It's like I am drawn to him. I don't know what it is." Jelena exhaled audibly, taking out her ponytail and ran her fingers through her hair. "Now, it's like I need to be with him."

"Escucha chica, if you feel so strongly about him just go after it."

"I have been married twice before Ang. Hell, I am technically still married to my 2nd husband," she groaned.

"Chica, whose book are you reading that says you can't be married more than once? Or you have to stay in relaciones abusivas but once you get married you have to stay married?"

Jelena's eyes began to water and Angela grabbed her by the shoulders and made her look her in the eye "Jelena, te quiero. Necesitas escribir tu propio libro, no leer de alguien más," <love you You need to write your own book, not read from someone else,> she said.

Jelena hugged her friend tightly,tears streaming down her face.

"Cassidy and I will be there, your house at 7 to get ready."

Jelena sniffled and wiped her face. "Thanks," she said.

\#

Saturday night Jelena opened her door and welcomed Angela and Cassidy in. She had already showered and was in shorts and a t-shirt.

"Hola," she said to Cassidy after she hugged Angela.

"Damn girl," Cassidy said. "This place is nice, must've cost you a fortune."

"Actually, I'm leasing," she responded and giggled when Cassidy's eyes got wide.

"Make yourself at home Cassidy; Ang and I are going to get dressed," Jelena said.

Angela grabbed her duffle bag and headed upstairs after Jelena to get ready for the party. They were dressed very casually, each of them with jeans and blouses on. Jelena was in the bathroom mirror finishing up her makeup and Angela was at the vanity in the bedroom doing the same.

"Are you nervous?" Angela yelled to Jelena.

"Maybe," Jelena yelled back.

Jelena walked out of the bathroom. "What do you think?" she asked, pointing to her face.

"Perfecta" Angela responded.

There was a knock at the bedroom door, and Cassidy stuck his head in. "I can't believe y'all actually took two hours" he teased.

Angela looked at him and smiled. Jelena rolled her eyes "Yeah, yeah, yeah, whatever."

Cassidy stepped further in the room. He stared at the girls with mock surprise, "You two spent all that time here and all y'all wearing is jeans and a t-shirt."

The two women giggled and the trio left to head to Jordan's house. Jelena went to turn towards the woods and Angela stopped. "Aren't we getting in the car?" she asked.

"It would be too much to drive, it is literally a two-minute walk. To drive we would have to go all the way around."

Angela and Cassidy were skeptical but followed. Once they arrived at Jordan's place, Cassidy looked at the place with awe. "All these houses are gorgeous," he said.

Jelena smirked and rang the doorbell. She was expecting a butler to answer the door. She was surprised when Jordan answered the door himself.

He grinned widely when he saw her, staring at her intently. She said hello, then began to blush when he didn't respond.

Angela cleared her throat, thinking it would break the trance. When that didn't work, she nudged Jelena making her jerk forward slightly. Jelena turned her head and scowled. Angela opened her eyes wide and tilted her head.

Jelena caught on to her mistake and looked back at Jordan. "You remember Angela?" while gesturing behind her "this is her boyfriend Cassidy Firestone."

Jordan broke his gaze and shook hands with her friends. Once he was done with the pleasantries, he opened the door and gestured for them to enter. "Make yourself at home."

When they were passing him he grabbed Jelena's bicep to hold her behind. She paused while Angela and Cassidy passed. When they were alone in the doorway Jordan grabbed her and pulled her close to him and leaned in close to her ear.

She melted into his body and wrapped her arms around his neck. His hands traveled down to the small of her back and pulled her closer.

Jordan kissed her, letting one hand travel up her back and became entangled in her hair, holding her head in place. The rest of the world floated away. There was nothing around but them and they were lost in the passion that enveloped them and sealed them off from everything else.

The ground shook, and Jelena snapped out her bubble. Her head jerked back, breaking the kiss, and she looked from right to left.

"Relax," Jordan said. "It's just my nephews and cousins banging around."

Jelena pushed slightly on his chest, creating a fraction of space between them. "How can a few boys make the ground shake?" she asked.

"A few boys couldn't," a grin spread across his face. "But a few wolves could."

Jelena rolled her eyes and smirked. The next moment her eyes got wide, and she gasped. "Cassidy doesn't know!" she exclaimed. "Cassidy, Angela's boyfriend, does not know you guys are shifters," she insisted.

Jordan ran his hand through her hair, pulling her close again. "He knows now. Relax, we don't eat people."

With the moment gone, she became self-conscious about how intertwined they were standing in the open doorway in a house full of people. Red faced, she pushed against him enough to separate them. Then she adjusted her jeans and blouse, unable to look him in the eye

Jordan caught on to her anxiousness. "What's wrong?"

She looked at him. "Nothing. Are you going to invite me in or am I stuck in the doorway?"

Jordan grabbed her hand and led her into the house.

The first hour went by in a blur. He introduced her to his aunts, uncles, brothers, sisters, nieces, nephews and cousins. There had to be over 100 people here. There was music playing and food available everywhere.

People and wolves alike were running around talking and laughing. She and Jordan settled in a corner with Johnathan and his wife along with Jordan's sister Amara and her husband. Jelena sat on Jordan's lap. Partly because he wouldn't let her sit anywhere else.

As she looked around the room, she spotted Angela and Cassidy sitting in another part of the house surrounded by Jordan's family. She started to tear up and blinked quickly to get rid of the tears.

Jordan began to rub his hand up and down her side. "What's wrong?" he whispered.

"Nothing," she shook her head. "You have a big and wonderful family."

The party didn't break up until well after midnight. The massive amount of food had been demolished. Jelena knew they would have healthy appetites, but she didn't know healthy meant massive.

Diane and Jordan's father, John, were left as well as Jacob, Jordan's eldest brother and his wife. Everyone was cleaning up.

Jordan grabbed Jelena by her waist and spun her around unexpectedly. She let out a squeal followed by giggling.

Diane sighed with happiness. She glanced at John who was not far and mouthed 'She's the one.' John rolled his eyes and abruptly headed for the door without speaking.

. Angela went up to Jelena. "We are going to walk back to the car."

"Okay, let's go," Jelena said.

Angela shook her head. "No tu, sólo nosotros."<No, you stay here.>

Jordan came up behind Jelena and wrapped his arms around her waist. "We have not got that far in my lessons yet, but I hope she said you stay with me."

Jelena looked at her friend skeptically "You sure?"

Angela looped her hand through Cassidy's arm and spun them around. "Sí chica, adiós" she replied and went around the room to say her goodbye.

Diane gave Jacob and his wife a hug and said their goodbyes. As Jelena went upstairs to shower, Diane took the opportunity to go talk to Jordan.

"Come here, son," she said.

Jordan walked over to his mother and leaned against a counter. "Why do I feel like I'm in trouble?" he said.

"Jelena is a very nice girl. I can see why you imprinted on her," she said.

Jordan rolled his eyes. "Always get tested and use condoms. We have had this talk all ready Mother."

"I haven't seen you this way with anyone else before," she stated bluntly, ignoring his comment."Once you as an Alpha has claimed her, appoint me to head the ceremony, so we can recognize the new luna.," his mother said more of a statement than a question.

"Claimed!" Jordan exclaimed. "Hold on mother, one step at a time huh."

"Mother sees all," she embraced her son and kissed him on the forehead. "Tell Jelena I said bye," and she left the house.

The Claim

Jelena got out of the shower. She wiggled her toes on the plush rug and took a deep breath taking in the softness of fabric beneath her feet. She tossed on one of Jordan's shirts, which fell down below her knees.

She pondered whether she should put back on her underwear. They were the only pair she had, not expecting to stay over. She remembered her Abuelita saying *nunca use su ropa interior dos veces, <never wear your panties twice>*. But what message was she sending if she didn't have underwear on?

When she walked out of the bathroom Jordan was in the bed on his phone. She walked over and climbed in the bed. Before she got comfortable, he grabbed her and pulled her face close to him so their lips met.

As their passion escalated Jordan felt an urge that drew him to her neck. Kissing, sucking and licking her neck, she thought he was going to give her a hickey. Then she felt a small pinch of pain that sent both of them over the top.

Jordan tore his shirt, shredding it to pieces. Happy to see she had nothing on underneath he devoured her mouth. Jordan hovered over her naked, pinned body.

She looked at him with lust-filled eyes. He kicked off his pants and bent down, kissing her neck again. Biting down, he broke the skin. Jelena cried out, not sure which sensation she was feeling.

As they continued to mate, Jordan became more and more fierce. She looked up at him, his eyes were completely gold. *A sign that the wolf is here* she thought to herself. Jelena lost herself in his gold eyes as he led her to ecstasy.

Jelena rolled over on her back struggling to catch her breath. "You bit me," she said as a realization dawned on her. "You marked me, claimed me," she said more urgently. She sat up in the bed and looked at him expecting an explanation. He was passed out, snoring lightly.

Unable to enjoy the moment, she lay back on the bed. He had made her the queen of his pack. *What have I gotten myself into, she thought?*

\#

Jelena lit up Jordan's phone again; it was 5 a.m. She didn't know where hers was. She put the phone down and sighed. Unable to sleep, he had been watching the walls for the past three hours.

Her mind whirled with the mark she was sure had material-ized on her neck. Frustrated by the situation, she decided to take a relaxing bath.

She turned on the water and thought she heard a noise. Sticking her head out of the bathroom, she heard a bump coming from somewhere in the house. Jordan's phone lit up and the sudden illumination caught her attention.

Going over to pick up the phone, terror flooded her when his phone said 'Alert, security breach,' blinking on the screen.

"Jordan" she whispered. When he didn't move, she said louder "Jordan." He stirred but did not move.

"Fuck" she said and went over to his closet,grabbed a pair of sweatpants and a t-shirt.. She pulled the drawstring as tight as it would go and slipped his phone in the pocket. She exited the closet and searched the dark room for a weapon. She had left all her essential things at her house.

"Stupid," she mumbled.

With nothing in sight she went to the bedroom door and slowly opened it. She poked her head out, turning it from side to side searching for intruders. The house was dark, so she was searching for shadows and signs of movement. When she believed she was all clear, she stepped in the hall. Her knees were bent, arms out loose to her sides. She hadn't explored Jordan's house yet, so she was unfamiliar with the layout.

At the staircase, she stopped to look around and to listen. She didn't hear anything or see any movement. She slowly walked down the stairs and paused again when she hit the bottom.

She decided to go towards the kitchen. Thanks to the party last night, she knew where that was and was familiar with the layout.

As she entered, she remembered she didn't have a weapon. She spotted the knife block. She didn't like to use knives; it was a great possibility that she would get hurt. On top of that, knives required close combat, and she liked to avoid getting close whenever she could.

As she approached the block, she felt a burst of wind on her back. Before she could turn a large forearm grabbed her around her neck. An arm came up and pressed against the fist that was choking her, applying even more pressure.

Jelena panicked and tried to scream but her attacker bent backwards, lifting her off the ground. Now she couldn't breathe, let alone scream. She grabbed and scratched on the arm tightening around her windpipe, flailing and kicking her feet.

The more she struggled, the less air she was able to suck in.

Tears started pouring down her eyes. She felt lightheaded and knew she would lose consciousness soon. *I have to get out,* she thought. All her maneuvers were worthless because her attacker had her off the ground. There was no way to gain any leverage. She started kicking her feet backwards, trying to catch him in the knees or the legs. He changed his position and began punching her hard in the abdomen. She stopped kicking immediately. He took her and slammed her head on the counter.

This left her dizzy; though he loosened his grip to hit her so she could breathe slightly. She greedily tried to suck in breaths, but couldn't exert that much energy and began to cough. The man stood back up, lifting her off the ground, and began choking her again.

Jelena's vision started to darken, and she knew she was losing consciousness. Before long, her vision was completely black.

Andre released the woman when he felt her go limp. She dropped to the floor with a thud, her head bounced a few times. He wondered who the woman was, if she was important to the youngest Romano brother, then killing her was icing on the cake.

Andre lifted his head slightly, smelling a different scent. He turned his head just in time to have a brown wolf jump on him. He fell to the ground, unable to shift.. The wolf tore apart the skin on his wrists and face, trying to get access to his neck.

The woman on the floor moved slightly, catching his attention and the attention of the wolf. Andre took that opportunity to push the wolf. A brown ball of fur went flying across the kitchen and slammed into the wall sliding until it hit the floor.

Andre got up and contemplated changing. He looked from the

wolf to the woman and both were unresponsive. "Jordan, here I come" he sang menacingly, blood dripping from his arms and his face. He turned and walked towards where he believed the staircase was.

He hadn't taken more than three steps when something hit him hard in the back of the head repeatedly. The vicious attack caught him off guard, causing him to fall to the ground and groan.

Jelena held the pan above her head and smashed it down over the man's face. She looked towards the crumbled wolf on the ground. The wolf was changing back into a human. "Diane," Jelena gasped and rushed over to her.

Neglecting her own injuries, she lay down besides Diane, weeping. She didn't know how to help.

"Stop that dear," Diane rasped. "I need to be in human form to heal. I'll be fine now.

Jelena took off the sweatpants and carefully slipped them on Diane. Diane gave little resistance. Jelena lay down on the floor, putting her head by Diane's head and her arm draped across Diane's bare breasts.

Her new injuries and her old injuries all were coming back full force. She lay on the floor unsure of whether help was coming. Remembering she had Jordan's phone in the pants pocket, she struggled to reach it. After a few moments, she gave up and her body went limp.

Five blurry, unfamiliar figures rushed into the kitchen. She was too hurt to be scared, and she wouldn't leave Diane. Right before she passed out she looked up and saw gold eyes.

I'm going to kill him

Jordan growled and rushed over to Jelena and his mother laying on the floor, with his father close behind him. "How could you have slept through this?" John barked.

Jordan growled. "Stop that, boys. John, you know how it is the mating night. You fell asleep and were dead to the world too," she admonished. "I'm healing, I will be okay, help Jelena."

The Romano brothers went over to Andre on the floor "We will take him," Jacob said.

"I'm going to kill him." Jordan rushed over, picked up Andre around the throat, choking him. His sister ran over to him grabbing him by the arm.

"Jordan, I need you to let him go. Please, let the boys handle him. Stay here with me and take care of mom and Jelena."

That snapped him out of his rage, enough to release Andre's neck. The man needed to rest so he could heal enough.

Jordan turned back to Jelena and his mother. John picked up his wife, preparing to carry her back to their house. He hesitated. "Take care of your mate and leave the hyena to your brothers. Alphas do not retain all responsibility, they delegate." With that he left.

Jelena stirred on the floor and groaned. Jordan rushed to her side, picked her up delicately, and laid her down on his bed. He went over to his drawer to get her something else to put on. Grabbing basketball shorts and another ,he went back over to the bed and undressed her.

He remembered she didn't have anything on under his t-shirt. Once he pulled it over her head, rage filled his body again as he saw all the bruises peppering her body. He saw the new ones created by Andre and the old ones spread across her abdomen. How could he have missed these before?

Not wanting to move her to put the new clothes on, he pulled the covers up over her.

Jordan stripped and climbed naked in the bed next to his mate.

\#

Jelena opened her eyes and looked at her surroundings, gathering her bearings. The last thing she remembered was her night with Jordan. She remembered feeling uneasy and overwhelmed afterwards but nothing else .

She stretched and immediately regretted that decision. She pulled back the confronter and gasped at her naked, purple body..

Jordan came rushing into the room. "Don't move," he ordered.

"How did you know I was going to move?" she whined.

"I've been listening for you," he said.

Jordan helped her lay back down. "You need to relax," he said.

"What time is it?" she asked.

"It's around noon," he said. "On Tuesday."

She bolted upwards. "Tuesday! I've been - what - sleeping since Saturday night?"

Jordan got into the bed next to her, draping his arm around her neck. "What do you remember?"

"I remember you marking me without my permission," she said, absentmindedly feeling the spot where he bit.

"You are upset that you are my mate?" he asked with an edge in his voice.

Jelena sat up and leaned against the headboard. A little self-conscious about being naked she grabbed the blanket and covered herself.. "I don't know exactly what that entails, plus I am still married. I wish you would've talked to me about it first," she sighed

"You plan on staying married to him?" he accused.

"No, I don't; but that doesn't change the fact that you made a really important decision about my life without me."

Seeming to relax a little at her revelation about going through with her divorce he asked. "What do you want to know?"

Jelena took a deep breath. She was better off getting all of her questions and anxieties out, it's not like she could just tell him to take his claim back. Sitting straight back so she could avoid eye contact she asked, "Am I going to have to be turned into a wolf?"

"Eventually," he said. "We have to wait for the blood moon. There is about another year or so for that. Is that going to be a problem?"

"Well, I've never thought about it," she huffed. "Last month I was an FBI agent who was married for almost two decades. My life was very simple. Since then I have been kidnapped, tortured, discovered my husband is a controlling, manipulative woman beater, and have gotten marked by a wolf. And not just any wolf, just my fucking luck that he's the Alpha of not only his pack but all the packs in North America. I have been choked and beat by God knows who because I decided not to go home, probably opening my old wounds. I don't even know what good going home would have done, that place got broken into before I even moved there!"

Jelena stopped and looked at Jordan for the first time. "Diane," she whispered. "How is Diane?"

"My mother is fine," Jordan said. "I can see why you are overwhelmed, I had no clue you went through so much in shit a short time."

"I need to see her," she declared. Jelena pulled back the covers and hopped out of the bed. She paused, her body protesting. Once she could move again, she went to the bathroom and put on the clothes she wore to the party.

It hurt for her to bend anything, dressing took longer than usual. Once she was finished she tentatively looked at herself in the mirror. Her face looked tired, but it wasn't bruised. She felt lumps on her head and her neck was bruised and sore.

She exited the bathroom to see Jordan had not moved from his spot.

"Don't you think we should finish this conversation?" he asked .

Jelena crossed her arms over her chest glaring at Jordan. "What is it you don't want me to see?" she asked him.

"There is nothing," he shrugged. "I just think this is an important conversation."

"I will knock on every door on this property," She turned and headed for the door. With incredible speed, Jordan got up before her, blocking her way.

"Okay," he conceded. "We will go see my mother. When we are done we will come back and talk, okay?"

"Fine," she said.

\#

John came and opened the door. "She's awake, good," he

bellowed flatly. Jelena was starting to realize that was normal for him.

"Is Diane okay?" Jelena asked anxiously.

"She is healed and is now resting. There is only one bedroom upstairs, you two can go up," he said, not acknowledging his son.

She noticed the strong animosity from John to Jordan. She made a mental note to re-approach that topic later.

Once upstairs Jordan opened the bedroom door. Jelena squeezed passed him. "Diane, are you okay?" she asked, rushing into the room.

Diane was sitting on the bed in a plush robe, watching tv. "Hello dear," she greeted Jelena sweetly.

Jelena rushed over to the side of the bed and then hesitated.

Diane held her arms out, inviting Jelena in for a hug. "I am completely healed."

Jelena fell into a hug, holding on to the other woman tightly. "I am so glad you're okay," she whispered .

Jelena took a step back, and Diane patted the bed. Jelena did as she was told and sat.

Diane looked at Jordan. "Why don't you go swim some laps dear."

Jordan hesitated in the doorway, and then turned and left, closing the door behind him.

"How do you feel?" Diane asked.

Jelena shrugged and looked down at her fingers. "Well, aside from being sore and probably internal injuries because I am sure some of my wounds opened back up; I am nervous, worried and scared." Jelena finished talking and closed her eyes briefly while she took a deep breath.

"First thing's first," Diane began. "What do you mean old

wounds?"

Jelena told Diane about Kinkcade and what she had been through. When she was finished with her story she said, "When whoever that attacked me..."

"There could be internal damage because you've had previous wounds," Diane finished. "Oh dear. I am so sorry that happened to you." Diane rubbed the back of Jelena's shoulder. Jelena couldn't bring herself to ask about the marking.

Diane, sensing her apprehension said, "Being a Luna is a big job, but it is also fun and rewarding. Take it from me, I know."

"I am technically still married," Jelena said. At Diane's confused expression, Jelena explained her relationship with Alejandro and then her recent problems with Dan. She even expressed her worry that Dan's unwillingness to sign the divorce papers.

Diane put her hand over her mouth. "Oh my word, you have gone through enough heartache for three lifetimes. You are an incredibly strong woman, and would make an excellent Luna."

"I don't even know what that means," Jelen grumbled..

"It is the same as any other position as leading for first women," Diane explained. "The only thing I think you would struggle with is the change. I know I did when John first changed me..You won't have to give up anything, not even your job."

"I just wish he would have given me a choice, or at least had this conversation with me before he bit my neck off," she said, leaning on Diane's pillow. She immediately regretted the bad attempt at a joke, but Diane laughed.

Jelena and Diane talked until they fell asleep. She was awakened by Jordan, "Time to go," he whispered. She looked over through her groggy eyes; Diane was asleep.

As they were walking back to Jordan's house he asked, "So can we go back and talk?"

"I have to stop by my place," she said firmly. "I need an overnight bag and we have work to do. Oh, and I need to go see my brother too."

They switched directions and headed to the renter house.

To catch a killer

Jelena made Jordan's house hers. She was in her own sweatpants and a tank top. She had her computer, tablet, notes and other important documents spread all along the bed. She was sitting right in the middle, and she hadn't moved for hours.

Michaels informed Monroe of what happened. He wanted to rush over there, but they stalled him. Cohert had no choice but to call him to tell him she was awake.

She forced Jordan to tell her about the guy who attacked her. His name was Andre Franklin, and he was a hyena shifter. The Romano family went to visit Africa when John was Alpha to try to form an alliance. While they were there, the Alpha's son was brutally killed, and it was believed that John was the one who did it. There was a hit put on John, but he got the upper hand and the other guy was badly hurt. The family had to rush out of Africa to avoid further retaliation.

Jordan explained the confrontation with Andre on his land and how he believed Andre was connected to the other six killers. He also had told her that he checked his security and saw it was Andre who broke into their house because Jordan left the doors unlocked.

I mean, who would break into here knowing who he is? she

thought. Jordan apologized for not waking up but explained the deep sleep after a mating ritual. She understood but still was annoyed.

Jordan went to go to his brothers to check on the Andre situation. When he returned he chuckled when he found Jelena in the same spot. She seemed to be in a trance so he decided not to disturb her. He stood in the doorway and watched her. She was beautiful. Her chocolate grown hair was up in a sloppy ponytail with two pens stuck into the ponytail.

He could see every speckle of green in her eyes from across the room. The sun from the balcony was streaming in and made her skin glisten when the rays hit her. He stared at the woman he had claimed, the woman he had made his mate and happiness enveloped him. He never thought he would settle down. He knew she lived a long life in a short time.

He wondered whether he marked her too early. He didn't explain anything to her. They did not know much about each other. Maybe he should've just dated her. The deed was done, so it was too late for second thoughts. It was a punch in the gut when she told him he should've asked her first. He was so caught up in the moment, he wasn't thinking. He did what felt right to him and he just assumed it felt right to her too.

Caught in his doubts, he didn't notice Jelena look up. Her face lit up in happiness, which made his heart melt. In that moment he knew he had to erase any doubts she had, because he had no plan of letting her go.

"Hey, there you are. Where's Michaels, is he close?" she asked.

"Is it time to work already?" he scowled. "It's always Michaels and Cohert when it is time to work."

"I texted him telling him to come over. I thought you two

were together and he would just tell you."

"He's coming," he said casually.

"You can sit over there," she said pointing to a corner on the bed that was void of the mess she had spread out.

Jordan chuckled and went to his corner. He glanced at the paperwork she had everywhere. Jordan's phone buzzed, and he pulled it out of his pocket. It was a security alert "Jonathan, or Michaels is here," he said.

A few minutes later he came into the bedroom with his hands over his eyes. "I am coming in," he said loudly. "I require all bodies decent and with all clothes on"

Jelena rolled her eyes and Jordan scoffed, "Whatever, just come on."

Michaels pulled the chair from the desk and brought it up to the end of the bed. He slid the paperwork in front of him over so he could place his files down.

"Alright Cohert, I'll start."

"Jane Hawthorne was the first victim. She was taking the trash out. Her and a close friend waited until the last minute to do the chore and had to do it in the dark. Her friend, Tyler Riley, stood at the door and watched Hawthorne run to the trash cans which were about 40 yards away from the backdoor. Tyler explained she started laughing and wasn't looking at her, when she brought her head back down she couldn't see her. She reported hearing noises and figured Hawthorne was trying to scare her. She called out a couple times and then went back into the house. The next morning she didn't see Hathorne and looked outside. She saw her body on the ground," Michaels said.

"Margarete Mathew's family and friends said she went out that night to an open mic night. No one wanted to go with her so she went by herself. She texted her mother when she got there around 9 p.m. Phone records show she ordered a Lyft at 11:30 pm. She was found a half mile away from the bar. There is no security camera on the route from the bar to where she was found. The Lyft driver said when he arrived at the location there was no one matching the picture was there waiting for him. He canceled the ride and moved on."

"Danielle Toppson was found in her bedroom. Her roommate was on a date and reported coming into the house around 10 p.m. She heard a noise from the bedroom and figured her roommate had company and forgot to close her door. She went to close it and saw a figure run and jump out the window. Instead of closing the door she opened it and that's when she found her roommate," Michaels continued.

"Michelle Clemonds was found out here in the woods. It was at the end of the property, approximately three and a half miles from this house. She was coming from a party, according to her boyfriend, at Giovanni's," Michaels said and then looked pointedly at Jordan.

"The boyfriend said that during the party he felt like they were having a good time. Clemonds disappeared for about four songs – that's the boyfriend's words – and when she came back, she said she was ready to go, abruptly."

Jordan looked at his brother, the rage building up in his stomach. "He raped her?" he accused in a low voice. "How many other girls were found in the woods?"

"Four." Cohert answered

"How many of the others are connected to Giovanni?" he asked again.

Cohert hesitated. Jordan said, "Just say it Jelena."

"All three of my victims are connected to Giovanni. He is a

part of Pet's Need Love Too. It is a volunteering organization that helps shelters and such. He knew Stevens and Ellps from that group and Hemmingway from school," said Jelena. "That makes four of the seven victims tied to Giovanni; Clemonds, Stevens, Ellps and Hemmingway," Cohert supplied.

"I have to check out that organization and see if my two victims are a part of that too," Michaels said.

"We know he did not kill Lisa, the hyena did. So are Giovanni and the hyena working together?" Jordan refused to respect Andre's name.

"Let's not jump to conclusions. The DNA is still being run. However, if it is a shifter, it will come back inconclusive," she said.

"That is only for full blood shifters," Michaels said. "If one of your parent's is a human, or a changed shifter, not born, you will have readable DNA."

"Which means if it is Giovanni killing these girls, we will have a DNA match. Steve is human," Jordan supplied.

"We are under the impression that the same killer killed each of the girls. That can't be the case with Giovanni in the mix," Cohert said, trying to get some tension out the room.

"Remember what Rodriguez pointed out," Michaels said. "Why did he just bite Hawthorne and tore apart the others? Maybe Giovanni did the first kill and Andre took over."

"Hold on," Jelena said, putting her hands up. "We need evidence. I think it's time I talk to Giovanni, alone," she said pointedly looking at Jordan. "We are waiting on DNA and Michaels need to see if his other victims have the same PET connection. I'm going to go into the office and see what the lab says. Let's plan for tomorrow having Giovanni and his parents come so I can formally question him, alone."

"Cool with me," Michaels said.

Jordan sat there, unmoving. She could tell he needed to get a handle on his anger before he spoke.

"In other news," Jelena said. "What's happening with Andre?"

Michaels hesitated and Jelena sneered. "Don't you dare ask him for permission first."

A smirk broke through the scowl and hard lines on Jordan's face.

"We still have him," Michaels began. "He's not talking."

"I want to go. I want to talk to him."

Jordan said, "No" at the same time Michaels said "wait" as both men sat up at attention.

"Oh, I'm sorry," Jelena sneered. "I wasn't asking." She turned towards Michaels and she crossed her arms over her chest. "Don't you have to listen to me?"

"I don't," Jordan interjected before Michaels could respond.

"You won't stop me though," she challenged.

Jelena hopped off the bed. She went over to the dresser and slipped her shoes on. "If no one will take me there, I'll go ask Diane" she said. She walked to the door without waiting for an answer.

Jordan cursed and mumbled under his breath. "Okay" he grunted and got up. When he approached Jelena, she had a wide grin on her face.

\#

Jelena approached a shack-like building a few hundred yards behind Jordan's house. She couldn't believe they described it as a shack. *I guess when you're a billionaire it would be a shack. Does that mean I am a billionaire?* she thought and then quickly pushed the thought out of her head.

Jordan put one hand on her shoulder. "Hold up," he said.

She stopped and turned to him to see his face set in stone, full of hard lines.

"I want you to be careful," he began. "Do not get too close, don't let him get into your head."

Jordan rambled on for another couple minutes but Jelena tuned him out. She knew Jordan and Michaels wouldn't let anything happen to her. Plus, she wouldn't be caught off guard this time if something happened. When he was finished she said, "Got it," and turned and walked into the 'shack'.

It was dark on the inside, something straight out of a movie. She couldn't make out any details anywhere, which was done on purpose she assumed. She was guided down some stairs and through a series of doors. No matter where she went in the shack, it was dark. They came to another door, and she bumped into Jordan's back. He had hesitated before opening the door.

"Oh, Dios mío," she said. "Warn me next time."

"Jelena, I really need you to be serious," he said, almost pleading with her.

"Isn't he injected with wolfsbane?" she asked.

He sighed. "Yes."

"And you will be in there with me, right?"

"Yes," he said again.

"So what do I have to worry about?" she asked.

"Just promise me," he said, ignoring her questions. "Please promise me."

Her heart sunk. That's what she was missing, he wasn't trying to be controlling. He was scared and worried about her. Her eyes welled up, she had never had someone scared for her before.

"I promise" she whispered.

Jordan took a deep breath and then unlocked the door. He stepped in first and blocked Jelena from seeing anything. The scent hit her first. It smelled like death. She couldn't believe that she forgot that they would be in here torturing him. She stood a deep breath to steady herself.

"We have some more questions for you, hyena" he spit out. Jordan hesitated a fraction and then moved to the side.

Jelena sucked in an involuntary breath. They had chained Andre by his ankles, and they hung up one in each corner of the room spread wide. He was suspended so high his feet were off the ground. There were cuts, bruises, and welts all over his body. His left eye was swollen, and there was blood dripping from his mouth and nose.

Jelena had to steel herself. She felt a flashback sneaking up on her. *This is not the time. Get it together* she scowled. Jordan was staring at her. She wasn't backing down, she would go through with this.

She walked forward and Andre lifted his head slightly. "Ahh, that's the new smell," he said. His head dropped back down as if it was too much energy to keep it up.

"That's what I smelled last night. It was faint then, but it's stronger now. You have recently been claimed." He attempted to laugh, but didn't have enough strength for that.

Jelena steeled herself. "Why were you in my house?" Her voice came out strong even though she felt a complete mess on the inside.

"Your house?" he asked. "Your smell was not through there. You sure he's telling you everything?"

Jelena kicked her right leg up, connecting with Andre's cheek, using her momentum to follow through and having both feet back on the ground slightly to the left of where she stood originally. She saw Jordan jerk out the corner of her eye. and then relax.

"I asked you a question," she said firmly. "I expect you to answer directly."

A flood of blood squirted out of his mouth and nose. He struggled to breathe for a few moments. Inside Jelena quivered. It wasn't too long ago where she was the one in chains.

She couldn't let that distract her so she pushed it down. She had to be intimidating. There was no room for memories here.

Once Andre stopped wheezing, and his breathing returned to the shallow breaths he said, "I was looking for him," he said, jerking his head towards Jordan, spitting out some blood..

"Why?" she asked.

"His father owes my father a debt. A son's life for a son's life."

"What proof do you have that John is the one responsible?"

"I don't need proof, my father said and so it is."

"My father never touched the Franklin boy," Jordan bellowed.

Jelena put her hand up behind her back and felt him take a few deep breaths. She noticed he was closer to her, no longer willing to hide in the shadows.

"My orders are to kill the youngest son," Andre said. "So I shall kill the youngest son."

"The youngest son is the Romano pack Alpha," Jelena said.

Andre's head jerked up and then hung back down. Fresh blood oozed from his face. He raised his head slower and held it up so he was looking her in the eye. "No," he rasped out. "The youngest son could not be the Alpha."

"Any son who challenges Alpha and defeats him will be named Alpha," Jelena said.

Andre let his head drop back low, "I did not know the youngest son was the Alpha son. I will accept my consequences from the council for attacking Romano Alpha."

Andre'sbody sank in defeat. The sound of the chains rattled Jelena, and her memories came surging back to the surface. She could no longer push them down so she turned and left the room. Once outside of the room she held on to a wall and doubled over. Her breathing quickened, and she felt nauseous.

She heard the door closed and Jordan's footsteps coming up behind her. He picked her up. "I am fine" she protested. "The chains brought back memories, that's all."

Jordan silently carried her all the way to the front door. Once there she began to struggle. "Let me down," she ordered.

"I will not come out of here with you carrying me. What if someone sees you?" she exclaimed.

Reluctantly Jordan put her down. She stumbled a bit when she was on her own two feet. She steadied herself before Jordan could help.

"What information did you get out of him?" she barked, pointing a finger in her chest..

When he didn't respond she said, "It must've been my smell." Thenshe turned and went back to his house.

Reunited

J elena was in her car driving to Oliver's house. She had called him and figured out he was home, not in the office. She told him she was on the way and he welcomed her eagerly. Once she pulled up, he was outside. *He must have been watching for me*, she thought. She took a few deep breaths to ready herself and then stepped out of the car. She plastered a smile on her face and walked forward.

When she reached the door, he enveloped her in a hug. She was stunned for a moment. Her and Oliver had not embraced each other in so long.

"Come in," he said. "We have to talk."

She followed him into the house, and he motioned for her to sit on a sofa. "Want anything to drink?" he asked.

Shaking her head, she took a seat on the cushion's edge,with her back straight, feeling uncomfortable here. She looked around and noticed not much changed since she was here last. The decor changed a bit, but not a lot.

Oliver came back into the room holding a beer. "You don't mind, do you?" he asked, shaking the can slightly.

"Nope, not at all," she responded.

He sat on the arm of a chair adjacent to her. "I can't help feeling guilty," he began. "I feel that if I had done better to support you through Alejandro. You wouldn't have been through the same thing with Dan."

It wasn't the same thing with Dan, she thought. "Why didn't you support me?" she asked instead.

Oliver took a deep breath, "Papí told me not to. He said you were exaggerating, and you needed to stick in this marriage."

"You saw the bruises," she said.

He hung his head, "I know. I tried to tell him that he just wouldn't listen."

"Why did you need his approval?" she asked, eyes welling with tears.

"It was early in my career. I needed him to progress," he said shamefully.

"I didn't have that option," she growled. "I got to where I am without you or him because the both of you turned your back on me when shit got tough."

Oliver bowed his head.

"Look at me," she yelled. "You are my brother. I came to you expecting help, and you didn't give me anything." Jelena was sobbing. "I had to start fighting back, only relying on myself because the two people I had to rely on left me. They said I was exaggerating and putting bruises on myself. They told me to suck it up and stop making him mad. They made it so controlling and manipulative men are what I became used to, what I expected for myself."

Jelena took a deep breath and she started coughing.

Oliver kneeled in front of her. He reached up and placed both his hands on her knees.

"There are no words to describe how sorry I am. I understand now how detrimental it was for you to be going through a traumatic event and not have a support system. I told myself lies enough times that I began believing them myself. I was not there for you in the past. If you could forgive me, I want to be there for you in the present and the future."

He had finally apologized. All Jelena wanted all these years was for her father and brother to acknowledge what they did and how it affected her. She knew the great Deputy Director Dominguez would never acknowledge he was wrong, but it felt good for Oliver to do so.

Oliver got up and went back over to the arm of the chair. "In the efforts of full disclosure," he began. "I've been talking to Ana." Oliver paused. "And our Mother."

Ana was the younger sister of Oliver and Jelena. When they were younger, their mother left their father and took Ana with her. Neither one of them have spoken to their mother, Jada, or Ana since then.

Jelena never knew why their mother left, but Oliver was older and he knew. Their father was married to the job. Once she got into high school, Oliver told her about how their father was cheating with escorts. He would be in the office all day and have women meet him in the nearby hotel after hours. By the time he got home, he didn't have anything left for his wife, let alone his kids.

Eventually, their mother could not take it, took Ana and left. The fact that their mother had a choice to take Jelena and Oliver and didn't, crushed Jelena, and then she met Alejandro and thought her world was changing for the good.

"For how long?" she asked in a hurt voice.

"A long time," he said flatly. .

"Why?" she asked.

"I was older," he began. "I remember how great of a Mother she was and all the mess our Father put her through."

"And that makes up for her abandoning two of her children?" Jelena asked, bitterly..

"She didn't think she could support three kids on her own," Oliver said defensively.

Jelena sucked her teeth and rolled her eyes. "She was a Mother, Oliver, she didn't have a choice. She shouldn't have had a choice on which children she was going to Mother. It was her choice to leave, take one child and never be heard of again."

Jelena shook her head as if she were trying to unscramble all the thoughts. "Answer this question; did you contact her or did she contact you?" she asked.

Oliver sighed heavily,"I contacted her."

Jelena decided not to push this subject, she didn't have it in her right now. "Good for you," she said. "I have to get to work, I will update you on my progress."

They both stood awkwardly for a few moments and they finally got close enough to hug. Oliver held on to Jelena tightly and whispered "I love you" in her ear.

All she could muster was, "Bye Oli, a nickname she gave to him as a kid. She hadn't called him that in decades. The sentiment was enough of a first step for him.

Finally, a night in

Jelena and Angela sat on Angela's couch with an array of snacks, a bottle of wine, and some movie playing in the background. They had been talking and laughing through two movies so far.

"How is the boyfriend thing with Cassidy?" Jelena asked.

"The boyfriend thing," she scoffed, rolling her eyes. "You make it seem, I don't know, bad."

"It's just," Jelena hesitated "how long has it been since you've had a boyfriend? Because *I* can't remember a time."

"Una momento. I have had boyfriends before. I just prefer having more than one at a time."

"What, right now you're seeing more than just Cassidy?"

"No," Angela squealed, slightly offended.

"You're giving me mixed signals Ang," Jelena said, matter-of-factly.

Angela re-adjusted herself on the couch. "Okay, I am seeing Cassidy exclusively. When we were talking about it, he did this turn your phone face down thing and I mentioned him having sex with other women and he glided over my comment. I've been obsessing over it for days. I just don't know how to think."

"You should be mad," Jelena exclaimed. "He shouldn't be sleeping with other women while you two are together."

"You don't understand," Angela began. "We just recently actually decided to - actually date - er be exclusive." Angela told Jelena about the dinner she had with Cassidy.

"So you never told him that you didn't want him sleeping with other people. Were you dating around?"

"No. Well in the beginning there were games, but we both played games. When I felt us getting serious, I stopped dating around. But he didn't."

"How was he supposed to know you were taking things seriously?" Jelena asked, playing Devil's Advocate.

"Because I felt it was something mutual I wasn't just making things up," Angela said, getting a little defensive.

"Angela, you are used to playing games in relationships. There is no way for someone to know how you feel unless you tell them."

"I am not used to playing games," Angela said, raising her voice slightly "I am capable of having a grownup relationship, contrary to popular belief."

"No, listen. I am not saying you can't have a grown up relationship. All I am saying is that you started your relationship with Cassidy as a convenient fling. You two were working a case and as a result spent a lot of time together. You two were seeing each other but seeing other people too. Then you decided to not see anyone else because you were really starting to like him. You never told him you didn't want him seeing anyone else, you just assumed he was doing the same thing. What actually happened when you told him?"

"He didn't deny sleeping with other people," Angela huffed.

"Angela, what did he say?" Jelena pressed, ignoring her attitude.

"He said he wanted to be with me," she shrugged her shoulders and looked away, embarrassed.. "That from now on we were exclusive."

"So, it *can* bug you that he was having sex with other people when you thought you two were only with each other. But, when you actually came out and said that he made his decision."

Angela was quiet for a few moments and Jelena wondered if she had incited a fight.

Finally, Angela said, "Well, I'm not the only one who is dating," she said with a laugh.

Jelena let out a small breath. She averted her own eyes, embarrassed by her relationship chaos. "Yea, well apparently I am a queen like person to a whole pack, and I am married to a man refusing to divorce me."

Angela almost leaped off the couch. "He imprinted with you?"

Jelena rolled her eyes and grinned. "You must have re-watched Twilight."

"Whatever it is called, he did it to you! You're going to be a wolf?"

Jelena mumbled, "Well at least someone is excited about it."

Angela settled down. "Wait, you're not on board?"

"I like him, a lot. But it seems like everything went too fast. I just realized that I wanted to divorce Dan and now I have all these new responsibilities with a new relationship."

Jelena shared her doubts about Jordan and how she was excited but scared of her new adventure. She did not want to have a hard divorce with Dan but the way he has been acting is leading her to believe that that might be the only option.

"You got to get a lawyer," Angela said as she went into the kitchen to grab another bottle of wine.

"Yeah, I just wish we could settle this without all the legal stuff involved. I mean aside from me not wanting the headache. Now with all this Alpha stuff, it will be unwanted attention."

"Well, from what I hear, your divorce will be the least of Jordan's worries when it comes to unwanted attention."

Jelena perked up, "What have you heard?"

"The whole Giovanni thing," Angela responded.

Jelena let out a breath she didn't know she was holding. "Yeah, he decided that he will not protect Giovanni. Plus, with a chance that Giovanni is somehow involved with this whole Andre thing."

Angela came back to the couch, "I didn't know about that development, spill."

Jelena told Angela about the possibilities with Giovanni being involved in the murders. They talked through the new bottle of wine.

"I think I need to call Jordan to come get me, you got me drunk," she said giggling.

#

"Did she tell you she didn't want it?" Jacob asked.

The brothers were at Jacob's house hanging out. Jacob's wife and kids were at a choral concert for his youngest son. The brothers had gotten together with the intention of talking about Giovanni and the mess he had gotten them into.

"How did we end up talking about me and Jelena?" Jordan rumbledg. "We are supposed to be talking about how to deal with Giovanni."

Johnathan looked up from his phone, putting it in his pocket. "I would much rather hear about you making someone the Luna of our pack who doesn't want to be."

Jordan ran his fingers through his hair. "She never said that," he argued.

"So what exactly did she say?" Jacob pressed.

Truth be told, he hadn't finished the conversation with Jelena so he really didn't know what she did or didn't want. He didn't know how she felt. He was already anxious enough with all the unanswered questions that he didn't want to hear all the mess he knew his brothers would say.

Sensing his unease Johnathan said, "Okay, so what are we doing about Giovanni?"

"If he is involved in all these killings I don't know what we are going to do." Jordan admitted, thankful for the change of topic.

"I need to be caught up," Jacob stated

"We have reason to believe that Giovanni is somehow involved in the Andre killings because all the victims are tied to him."

Jordan interrupted Jonathan. "All of them, you confirmed that?"

"Yeah, I did that today. They were all a part of PET." He turned towards Jacob and continued. "The first killing was really brutal and the rest didn't follow the same pattern., which is suspicious and could indicate two killers. Jelena has DNA being ran, if they come back inconclusive than it is a possibility they are from Andre, but -"

"If a profile comes back, then it can be matched to Giovanni because he isn't a full blood," Jacob interrupted. "What ties Giovanni to Andre?"

"Jelena's looking into that. I am supposed to talk to Giovanni and Amara to find out what I can without showing our hand," Jordan said.

"Hold on," Johnathan said, putting one of his out. "Giovanni and Amara are coming into the Bureau building tomorrow for

Jelena to interview."

Jordan chuckled. "Oh yeah, that's what I meant."

"Jordan do not go talking to them about anything yet, seriously. That could seriously mess up our investigation."

"Screw the investigation, let's just handle this in the pack," Jacob argued. "No need to even get the council involved let alone the police."

"It is already a police matter Jacob," Johnathan said. "If we would have caught on to it first, we could have kept it quiet. But, we didn't and as a result we have to follow the police route. Police do the investigation and police do the punishment."

Jacob scoffed. "That.'s stupid. Jordan, just tell that new girl of yours to drop it."

Johnathan and Jordan both chuckled. "Yeah, okay," they said in unison.

Jacob didn't understand what the big deal was. "Just let me go to Giovanni and figure out what is what. I'll handle it."

Jordan looked at his brother "Naw man. Like Johnathan said, this is past us, it's a police matter and we will let the police handle it. That's what I was going to do with Giovanni, anyway," Jordan scoffed irritated. "He got too damn comfortable with all his shit being erased. Living by the old rules created a fucking predator." Jordan slammed his fist on the side of the chair he was in, leaving a fist-sized dent.

Jacob grunted. "Watch the furniture bro. Olive is going to kill me for that." Jacob pulled out his phone and sent a text to his wife. Then he looked at Jordan. His brother was really upset. Giovanni really messed things up. Jordan had better things to worry about. He had to fix this for his brother, he would do it better than the police.

You have the right to remain silent

The next morning Amara, Steve, and Giovanni walked into the bureau building. Amara was scared. How this was an FBI problem and not MDPD, and, why hadn't Jordan said anything to her about this? Was she just doing them a favor now that she was in the family? There was something wrong, and it had her senses on edge.

The lady at the front desk told them to have a seat. A few moments later Jelena walked into the waiting area. She was smiling but Amara detected her heartbeat quickening. *Something is definitely up* Amara.

Jelena walked up to Amara and then Steve and stuck her hand out. "Hey," she said, trying to keep everything casual. She reached for Giovanni to shake his hand too but he had his hands buried in his pockets and did not budge.

"Okay then," she said. "Follow me this way."

They began walking to the elevator. Once inside, Jelena decided to do a more formal introduction. "My last name is Cohert. My title here is Senior Agent. I've been doing this for almost two decades"

They exited the elevator and went to an interrogation room.

"So what, are you doing Uncle J a favor or something?" Giovanni asked.

Jelena waved them into the room and indicated for Giovanni to sit in the chair at the table. There were two more chairs in the room. One for the interrogator and only one extra one. Steve let Amara sit as he stood behind her.

"I am very aware," Jelena began. "That there is some conflict of interest here. To cover all of our bases, I have pulled Agent Chad Belle to act as lead interviewer today." Belle entered the room, and Jelena stood up giving him her chair. She went and stood against the wall directly behind him.

"What's a conflict of interest?" Giovanni asked.

"She can't ask the questions because she's our Luna," Amara spat.

Jelena jumped in. "The fact that I am dating your uncle makes people question my objectivity. Belle is here because he is an objective person who can conduct this interview."

"What's this all about?" she asked looking back and forth from Belle to Cohert.

"How often do you throw parties?" Belle began, ignoring her question.

Giovanni was caught off by the question, Amara was too. She was expecting them to dive into the rape allegations.

"I - Uh, I have friends over a lot. We have a big family so if we all invite friends over, it turns out to be a lot of people."

Jelena noted he didn't answer the question directly. She wanted him to say on the record that he was the only child. Solidifying that he had a big extended family, not immediate.

"How many siblings do you have?" Belle asked. Jelena almost smiled at how good he was. She didn't tell him what to ask.

"I'm the only child."

"So when you say you have a big family you are talking about your cousins, because you are the only child? That would make your family only three people right?"

"We all live on the same property, that makes it easy to go from house to house and hang out. My Uncle Jordan owns the entire woodland grove area and we all have houses on that property, even her." he said, pointing to Jelena.

Jelena suppressed an eye roll and said aloud, "For the record I am a leasing tenant of Jordan Romano residing on the woodland grove property. I am approximately a half mile away from Jordan Romano's house and a mile and a half away from Giovanni's house."

"Giovanni," Amara hissed, giving Jelena a dirty look. "Only answer the question they are asking, nothing extra." Amara crossed her arms. She sensed something was wrong, that this was bigger than she originally thought.

Jelena foresaw Amara being a problem. She took a deep breath and calmed her breathing and by extension her heart rate. She felt stupid not realizing that Amara could sense her nervousness.

"Are all the parties that you have a lot of with your cousins and friends, always at your house? Or since you all live so close are they at a different house each time?" Belle continued.

"They are at my house."

"Are your parents always present?"

"No, they have -" Amara glared at Giovanni and he immediately stopped talking. "No," he said.

Jelena noted that she wanted him to only answer what was asked. Usually people don't know what to say. She found it odd that Amara not only knew that, but gave the advice to her son.

"Why not?" Belle asked, catching on.

"They have work and stuff and they go to Uncle Jordan and Nonna's house a lot. I'm a junior in high school. I don't need to be babysat. Plus, I can take care of myself."

"If I am correct, you have a lot of parties at your house with your cousins and friends without parental supervision."

Giovanni looked away. "It sounds like I'm doing something wrong when you say it."

"Is that a yes?" Belle asked.

"Yeah," Giovanni mumbled.

"Okay, tell me about Michelle Clemonds."

Jelena was staring at Giovanni, gauging his reactions. His eyes slightly widened and then went back to normal. It was so quick that she would've missed it if she wasn't looking for it.

"I think I know her from school, I can't be sure though. I'm popular so everybody thinks they know me," Giovanni replied.

"Wait, what does this have to do with Lisa?" Amara asked.

"Ma'am," Belle said politely. "Are you stopping this interview with your son?"

She jerked back slightly and looked at Belle suspiciously. "No," she said.

"Then please let me ask the questions. That way we can be done in a reasonable amount of time." He looked back at Giovanni. "Michelle took some Facebook pictures at a party at your house a few months ago."

"A lot of people come to my parties."

"So, you have so many people come to these unsupervised parties that you don't know everyone who attends?"

Giovanni's eyes darted between his mother and Belle. This guy was making him and his mom sound ridiculous. He kept saying unsupervised and why was he bringing up Michelle? This was supposed to be about Lisa.

"Giovanni," Belle prompted.

"I don't know her. She came to the party, we hung out, and

she left. That's it."

"I'm confused," Belle said with mock confusion on his face.

"Confused about what?" Giovanni asked. When Belle didn't answer immediately Giovanni turned to his mother. She stared at him. "Giovanni you need to tell the truth."

Giovanni shrugged his shoulders. "I am, Mom," he snapped.

"Watch you tone with your mother," Steve said, speaking for the first time.

Amara continued as if Steve hadn't spoken. "First you said you don't know if you know her from school, that you're so popular everyone knows you. Then she was at our house, but you have so many people in the house when I am not there you don't remember. Then you hung out with her, and she left. You just told three different stories. Tell the truth!" she yelled.

That puzzled Jelena. Amara acted as if she didn't know her son had these parties. At the least she didn't know what he and his cousins were doing when the adults were somewhere else. But before she was acting protective trying to lead the interview. That was in direct contrast to how she was acting now telling him to tell the truth. Jelena made a mental note and re-focused on the interview.

Giovanni was upset his mother had yelled at him. His fists were clenched. "I know her from school, I invited her to my unsupervised party, and we hung out," he yelled.

Amara slapped Giovanni across the face. "Don't you ever speak to me like that again" she said in a low growl.

Giovanni sat there huffing, and puffing. He turned in his chair and faced Belle. "Are we done?" he grunted.

Belle sat there looking unaffected by the scene that just played out in front of him. "Tell me about the PET organization?"

Giovanni was taken off guard. He answered hesitantly, "We

meet every week. We volunteer at pet stores and shelters and stuff."

"And that's where you met Jane Hawthorne, Margrette Mathews, Danielle Toppson, Frances Stevens, and Tonya Ellps, right?"

Giovanni's eyes bugged out of his head as he shot straight up. "I want a lawyer," he shouted.

"Wait, what," Amara said confused. "He is a minor, we work in his best interests. Who are those girls?"

Belle kept firing off questions. "What was it Giovanni, Jane gave you so much trouble you told Mr. Franklin you couldn't do it again?"

"Franklin, what the hell is going on?" Amara said, her voice rising. She was confused. What did Franklin have to do with anything?

Belle didn't miss a beat. "So you found the girls and raped them. Rape seems to be your thing. Then you would call up Mr. Franklin and tell him where to find the girl and he would take care of the rest, you know since you didn't have the stomach."

Amara stood up. "Wait what is this? Stomach for what, this isn't about Lisa. Someone better tell me what's going on right now," She said glaring at Jelena.

Jelena watched the scene play out. Amara had switched from tell the truth back to protective mom.

Belle continued, "See you're so used to your Uncle cleaning up your messes you don't know how to clean up after yourself." Belle raised his voice. "We have your semen in seven murdered girls. We have your DNA on Jane Hawthorne's neck and upper body where you slashed and cut her."

"Lawyer!" Amara yelled furiously. "This is over, get us a lawyer."

Belle looked back at Jelena, and she nodded her head. Belle stood and knocked on the door. Two uniformed officers came in and stood by the door. Jelena stepped forward and said, "Giovanni Romano, you are under arrest for the rape and murder of seven women. You have the right to remain silent, anything you say can and will be used against you in the court of law."

As she finished his Miranda rights Giovanni began shouting, "He said I was helping the pack. Everyone sees Uncle J as soft and I was helping his image." He looked at his mother. "I only killed one oMom, he told me to but I couldn't do all of them, I just couldn't."

"Stop talking Giovanni, stop!" Amara shouted over him.

Giovanni was taken out of the room and Amara scowled at Jelena. "You pop up and you ruin our lives."

Jelena did not back down. "Your son has been a predator since he hit puberty. These women died one each month for the past seven months. The predator you raised turned into a serial killer as his New Year Resolution, that had nothing to do with me."

Amara growled and stepped in her face. Jelena knew she couldn't take her with brute strength, but she hoped all her years of training gave her an edge.

"Cohert," Belle said, trying to eliminate the hostility.

She ignored him, not willing to step down as a woman or as the new Luna to her pack. Then she heard that deep voice that had an instant calming effect on her.

"Challenging your Luna comes with consequences," Jordan said.

Amara stood there a few more moments and then turned to him. "You were here the whole time. Why didn't you stop this?" she demanded.

"I said I would not be providing any protection," Jordan replied calmly.

"They arrested him for murder, saying he is a serial killer. This is way bigger than rape! He did it for you. He was manipulated, he said - he said," Amara had to stop and catch her breath.

Jelena spoke up, determined not to be shut down by Jordan's presence. "If helping Jordan was all it was about, murdering the girls would've been enough. He didn't have to rape each one before they died."

Amara deflated. "My son may need some help but he is not a murder."

Steve, who was behind Amara the whole time, put his hands on her shoulder. "We have to go, we need a lawyer. Jordan isn't going to help so we are on our own."

You failed as a parent

J elena was in her office with her head leaned back against her chair. That whole encounter was stressful. Balancing these two roles is going to be harder than she thought. Her doorknob jiggled and then there was a knock at her door. She got up and smiled when she saw Jordan standing there. Leaving the door open she went back to her chair.

"You're going to have to punish her for challenging you," he said coolly.

"What type of punishment?" she asked, feeling anxious.

"We can talk about that later. Amara is coming in, she has questions about where he is being held and frankly I do not know."

She nodded and took a deep breath. Jordan opened the door and Amara walked in. "Steve is calling a lawyer," she said, without being prompted. "He can't be held in jail, he will break out."

"There is a facility that holds shifters. The inmates can make one phone call a day, only outgoing calls." Jelena remained sitting behind her desk.

"How will it hold them?" Amara asked.

"The bars are made of silver. The food is laced with wolfsbane. Just enough to keep everyone there controllable and unable to shift. The handcuffs are laced with silver. Each inmate needs to be shackled and handcuffed when they leave their cell."

Amara looked like she was going to cry. She took a moment to process and the horror on her face intensified. "Will he be in a juvenile section?"

"There is no such thing," Jelena said coolly.

"My poor baby," Amara began. "He doesn't deserve this. He was coerced, he was manipulated," she turned towards Jordan. "Joran please, please help. Don't let your nephew go to a place like that."

Jordan stared at his sister sorrowfully. "It is unfortunate that Giovanni has gotten himself entangled in something of this magnitude."

"You're going to say no, I don't want to hear anything if you're going to say no." Amara began crying. She backed up against a wall and sank all the way down, hitting the floor. "My son is going to be eaten alive."

Jelena's heart broke. She hated seeing Amara, or any mother for that matter, on the floor crying because their son was going to jail. She would not disagree with Jordan here; but she made a mental note to ask him about this later. *How many arrests does Giovanni really have? She* thought.

"Amara" Jordan whispered. Hearing Jordan's voice pulled Jelena from her thoughts. Amara got up off the floor, her make-up was smeared, and she rubbed vigorously trying to clean up her face. She stepped towards Jordan, "I can expect this from her, not you, this is your nephew."

Jordan sighed and ran his hands through his hair. "Amara, if we would have properly disciplined him instead of just making the problems go away he would not be a predator now."

"My son might need help but he is not a predator," Amara

said defensively.

"How can you say that?" Jordan roared in frustration

"Jordan, predators can't be fixed, that does not describe my son."

"Yes, it does. Every time some girl pressed charges or his DNA turned up in an investigation, either me or John made it go away. After all these chances he did the very same thing time after time. He had the space to learn and grow and decided not to. The two of you as parents failed every time he offended again. You took advantage of John and I by not working on your son and relying on your Alpha to erase your problems."

Jelena gasped audibly at the harsh words. Jelena wondered why he hadn't been punished or rehabilitated in the past. She didn't think sex offenders could be rehabilitated but obviously Amara did. So why didn't she try to help her son?

Amara looked at Jordan with hurt in her eyes. "You have no right to judge me until you have kids of your own."

Jelena's eyes got wide. She didn't want kids, and she definitely didn't want wolf kids. Could she even have kids with a shifter if she was human?

"It is my job to keep the entire pack's interest in mind. Ours, as well as all the packs in North America. Covering up the secret didn't work, now it is time to make an example and teach a lesson."

"Why does Giovanni have to be the example?" Amara yelled.

"He is the one with the unacceptable behavior," Jordan replied calmly, mimicking his father slightly.

There was a knock at Jelena's door, and then it opened without waiting for a response.

"Un momento," she began as Monroe's head popped through the door.

"When you knock you wait for a response," she told him in Spanish.

"Your brother does, your boss doesn't which I am in this setting," he responded to her in Spanish. "Cohert, I hear you made an arrest, I am here for an update," he said switching gears from informal to professional, from Spanish to English.

Monroe walked in the room and shut the door behind him. He walked up to Jordan and extended his hand. He turned to Amara, "I don't think we've met," he said, extended his hand.

Amara looked him in the eye, ignoring his hand. "Who are you?"

The astonishing disrespect pissed her Cohert off. "Mrs. Romano, I believe this man asked you a question. And before you answer I would remember the position you and your family are in and think about how you do not have room to be disrespectful to anyone in the building let alone the Assistant Special Agent in charge."

Amara looked at Cohert, and Cohert gave her a look daring her to continue with her blatant disrespect. Amara shut her eyes and took a deep breath. When she opened them, she was looking at Monroe. She stuck her hand out. "Hello, I am Amara Romano, you people just arrested my son."

"I am Oliver Monroe, AC - well she just told ya', no use for me saying again that I am her boss's boss," Monroe raised his eyebrows making sure she understood that friends were what she wanted out of him, not an enemy. He shook her hand. "So you are Giovanni's mother?"

"May I be excused?" Amara asked Cohert through clenched teeth.

Cohert was so mad she almost growled. She was so used to being in the Alpha family, with the Alpha's sister, being on top.

"Yes."

Once Amara left Monroe turned towards Cohert, "What do you got?"

Cohert told him the evidence she had against Giovanni, Andre Franklin confessed, and he was transported to the shifter facility.

"Alright you two," Cohert said, while walking back to her desk. "Let me get work done, I still have to prepare this case to be handed over."

"You also need to discipline Amara, those are a part of your new duties. You need to plan Sunday dinner. We have a family dinner each Sunday. My mother has been planning it but that is a part of your duties."

Monroe looked confused. "What do you mean a part of her duties?"

Jordan looked at Monroe and then back to Cohert. "You also need to catch your brother up." Jordan kissed her forehead.

Cohert looked down at her buzzing phone. It was Dan "I also need to get divorced," she mumbled.

Jordan and Monroe turned and looked at her. "What?" they said in unison.

"Monroe, Jordan marked me. Jordan, I will call Diane for help because my ex husband is not going to divorce me. Now get out so I can get to work. I'm going to be here all night."

\#

Giovanni sat in the 10 by 10 cell, looking at the ceiling. The handcuffs, bars and doors were made out of silver. The food made him sick, but he had no choice but to eat it. He couldn't shift, something in the food maybe. His pod was never quiet. They always yelled, screamed, and growled. They taunted him and called him names. They made the wolf bubble up inside him. He paced the small space over and over.

He had one hour for rec where he and the others in his pod were let out of their cells. He never had to fight before. He was a Romano, no one dared to challenge him. In here, Romano didn't mean anything. He swore his name was the reason so many people bothered him in the first place. He hadn't been here two days yet and had been to medical three times. All they did was make sure no injury was bad enough to not self-heal and sent him back.

As soon as he got back, he got beat. How many times in an hour can he get beaten? These men were big and smelled like animals. He had rough-housed with Uncle J before, but that was just to work on his technique. Uncle J never gave him his full strength.

How could his mother and Uncle J let him come here? He bet it was the new Luna Jelena. He didn't want to kill them girls. That's why he only killed one, Andre killed the rest. He was scared at first and then hesitated. Andre was in his ear, barking at him to finish the job and he just went wild.

He did it to help Uncle J, to build his rep. People were saying that the Romano Alpha was a weak leader, *Other packs are saying your Alpha is weak* Andre told him.

He spoke to his lawyer when he first got here. She told him Andre had manipulated him, played him, that Andre believed Nonno was still the Alpha. She asked him all these questions and said that since Andre never said Jordan specifically, just your Alpha, we can't be sure who he was talking about.

She said his DNA was all over every girl, that the plan now was to get the jury to see him as a kid making a mistake. She said he was gullible, and Andre manipulated him.

He was a Junior in high school, not some gullible kid. Those girls got what they deserved. They were always all over him, texting him, and calling him all the time. Giovanni got up and angrily began to pace the room. Screw his mother and Jordan for letting him come here. All Jordan had to do was say the word -

"Romano, you got a visitor, come cuff up." He was interrupted by a guard.

Giovanni hated this, cuffing up. He had to go to the bars and lay his hands on the silver in order for the guards to put the cuffs on. He didn't believe he even had a visitor, the guards just wanted to take him somewhere, in some blind spot so he could be beat again.

"Naw, fuck that man, leave me alone."

"Giovanni, come cuff up," the guard yelled louder.

Giovanni looked at the guard and four others had come and stood behind him. They couldn't hurt him like the inmates, they would lose their jobs.

"Leave me alone," he said louder.

"I think he is refusing a direct order," the guard said. All the men behind him nodded and chirped in agreement.

The guard opened the door. "Come here and cuff up boy." The guard glared at Giovanni, cracking his knuckles.

Giovanni let out a loud roar and faced the guards, ready to change. They came rushing into the cell, and as Giovanni hit the concrete floor, he remembered they did something to stop his shifting. He couldn't shift and there were too many of them to fight back and laid there while they beat him. When they were done they turned him over and cuffed him. The silver burned his wrists.

"Better be glad you're leaving, you rapist," one guard whispered in his ear.

Giovanni got to the front. Jacob was standing there. Jacob became enraged; Giovanni had bruises all over his face. One of his eyes was swollen shut. His jumpsuit was all ripped, and he was bleeding all over.

"Who did this to you?" he asked, looking him over. "Are you badly hurt?"

"Nothing accelerated healing won't fix," Giovanni mumbled through swollen lips.

The officers released the handcuffs exposing the burn marks around his wrists. The guard shoved the discharge papers at him. "Better keep the rapist away, he won't last if he comes back."

Jacob looked at him with fire in his eyes, cracking his neck from side to side. His hands clenched into fists, and the veins in his neck popped. He was ready to change.

"All you animals do is rely on shifting," the guard said, then walked away.

"They give us something to stop us from shifting, I bet they give it to visitors too," Giovanni mumbled.

Once in the parking lot Jacob turned to Giovanni. "G, you need to run. If Jordan finds out I bailed you out, he will only get his girlfriend to bring you back."

He reached into his car and grabbed a duffle bag, filled with clothes. Then grabbed his wallet out of his pocket and pulled out a wad of money, shoving it towards him..

"Uncle Jacob, what's this? I don't understand."

"You need to run until this whole Andre thing is cleared up. We have to figure out a way to change Jordan's mind and have him help you. There was no way your parents, or I, were leaving you in there."

Giovanni stood there barely containing the panic. "Uncle

Jacob," he stammered.

"Take this stuff and go!" Jacob yelled.

Giovanni grabbed the bag and money. "How long until I am able to shift again?"

"I don't know, I don't know what they did to get you to stop."

Jacob patted Giovanni on his shoulder making him wince slightly. "I love you G, I will find you when this is over."

Giovanni began to tear up, he didn't wipe his face because his wrists, arms and face hurt. He looked at Jacob one more time and then turned and walked away.

Jacob stared after Giovanni and then opened his car door. Right before he got in, a scent caught his attention. He looked around, and even with his enhanced sight he didn't see anyone or anything. Tilting his head and inhaling deeply he identified the smell as cigarettes.

Jacob scanned the parking lot again, slowly this time. When he found nothing he hesitated slightly before getting in his car. He pulled off, not seeing the man come out from behind a tree. The man dropped his cigarette and stomped it out with his foot.

Attacked, again

J elena felt like it's been years since she slept. With solving the serial killer case and spending all night and all the next day preparing the case all she wanted to do was crash. She had just finished meeting with Rodriguez and Monroe which took forever and she had to re-do a lot of aspects of the case file. She hadn't been home in two days, sleeping in her office.

She pondered whether she should just go to the rental house. She had no energy for the fight with Jordan if she went back there instead of sleeping with him. She pulled up to his house and parked the car. She knew the sensor would tell him someone had arrived. She still didn't like the no keys and no locked doors thing, but she understood why he wouldn't need normal security precautions.

Stepping into the house, she dropped her bag and shoes right next to the entrance and closed the door, making a beehive to the bedroom. She walked over to the bed, stripping as she went.When she finally made it to the bed, she collapsed wearing only her underwear.

Jelena fell asleep immediately, she was exhausted, so exhausted she didn't notice someone hiding in the closet, she didn't hear the door open or someone creeping towards her. So exhausted she didn't notice the danger she was in until she was lifted out of her bed and a rope placed around her neck.

Immediately awake, she grabbed at the rope around her neck. She was panicking and scratching, her legs flailing around. Her brain shouted at her, *You're not helpless, don't act helpless.* Jelena forced herself to calm down, relaxed each of the muscles individually, feeling each one release tension.

Her limbs stopped flailing about. She reached up and grabbed her attacker's face scratching their eyes until she felt the inside of the socket. The attacker screamed, and the rope eased. Taking a deep breath, she slipped her wrist inside of the rope and slid it off her head.

She spun and took three steps back, getting in her protective stance. She finally got a look at the person who attacked her. Most likely male, over 6 feet. He was wearing jeans, a black hoodie and a ski mask. White, and his eyebrows were brown, which meant so was his hair. Jelena watched him, and he held his face, and then he looked up at her. His eyes were red, but they looked to be intact. *Please god don't let him be a shifter* she thought. There was no way for her to beat a shifter without her gear, which was in the trunk of her car.

He ran towards her hands outstretched. Jelena ducked below his arms and ramped her shoulder into his stomach. He grunted and punched her back twice and then grabbed her waist, picking her up off the ground. Jelena slipped her arms through and threw her weight towards the ground. The move caught him off guard and once her arms touched the ground she kicked backwards in his face three times. Her attacker groaned and stepped back holding his face. Jelena brought her feet back down and stood up. Then, he charged forward and kicked him in his stomach. Once his hands dropped, she lifted her leg and kicked hard in his already damaged face.

The man's head jerked back, and he stumbled towards the door. She was considering going after him but her adrenaline was overtaken by her exhaustion and now sore body. Jelena plopped down on the bed and ran her hands through her hair. She felt her neck, positive that if there weren't ligature marks there now, there would be pretty soon. Her back was sore as she had her hands on her hips and she stretched from side to side.

She hated that he didn't lock his doors and had all the security alerts go to his phone. She hated being attacked where she was supposed to feel safe. She hated being helpless in this shifter world.

"Where the fuck is he?" she mumbled.

She looked around for her phone and realized she left her purse by the front door and then yelled, "JORDAN!" at the top of her lungs.

Jordan arrived at his house and spotted Jelena's shoes and purse scattered across the front entryway. He went up to his room and found her pacing back and forth in the bedroom.

"¿Dónde está tu teléfono?"

"Uhh– my Spanish lessons tell me you said something about my phone." He patted his pants and when they came up empty, he said, "I must have left it at Jacobs, that's where I've been. Today is our movie night."

"¿Dónde está tu computadora?"

"So, we are continuing the lesson. Um, you said my computer, where is my computer," he shrugged. "I don't know, maybe downstairs."

"Ve a buscarlo."

"Okay now you've lost me."

"Go get your damn computer!" she shouted.

Jordan went to get his computer confused. He grabbed in and headed back to the bedroom trying to figure out why he was in trouble. He had barely seen her the last two days, what could he have possibly done.

He entered the room and sat on the edge of the bed. Jelena was still pacing back and forth. "You going to sit?" he asked.

"Open it," she said, while continuing to pace.

Jordan complied and powered on his computer. Once it was on he got a notification alerting him, his security had been breached twice today. He clicked on the notification figuring he would check out who else came to his house. He knew Jelena was one but was curious about who the other one was. His front door captured a picture of someone in a ski mask. Jordan frowned,checked the time stamp, and then checked the next breach. It was a picture of Jelena.

"Someone entered the house two hours before you came home. Don't worry I'll find out who was snooping around."

"Snooping around," she shouted. "Check the video."

"Just tell me what is going on Jelena."

"Check the damn video," she said slowly in a low voice.

Jordan sighed heavily and went back to his computer. He pulled up the video and followed his intruder through his house into his bedroom. He didn't have any cameras in his bedroom so he continued watching the one on the bedroom door and fast forwarded. The next time he saw anyone bother the bedroom door was Jelena. That didn't make any sense, he didn't see the intruder come out. He must've missed it because there was no way he was in the room when Jelena got home.

A few moments later, the man came stumbling out of the bedroom. Jelena watched his face and knew the exact moment when realization hit. "Why the hell aren't you paying attention to your phone when it went off, alerting you that man entered the house."

Jordan stood up. "Jelena I will."

"I don't want to hear what you're going to do. I want to hear why you knew some strange man came into this house and let me walk in after him and yet again fight for my life."

Jordan finally noticed her blood-shot eyes, the bruising around her neck. She was in her bra and panties. His face dropped, guilt filling in the lines that appeared.

"You know I contemplated going to my house. But I was too exhausted to argue with you about why I slept there instead of here. So I came here, so sleepy, and I came and I went directly in the bed figuring wherever you were you seen that I had come. What the hell is the point of having alerts go to your phone if you don't look at your damn phone. I am so helpless in your world. The only protection I have is you, and you fail over and over again."

Jelena grabbed her clothes off the ground and hurriedly put them back on. Jordan stepped towards her and she put her hands up. "Stop," she said. Jelena left the house and got in her car.

\#

Jelena pulled into Diane driveway and turned her car off. She sat there for a moment, unsure. She should've called first, on the way back from Angela's she thought about it. She had almost talked herself into going home when the front door opened. Diane stuck her head out and waved Jelena in. Jelena took a deep breath and got out of the car.

When she stepped up to the door Diane pulled Jelena into a hug. This woman made her feel so at peace. It was weird for her to connect with someone so quickly. Jelena scoffed to herself, *except Jordan* she thought *I guess it runs in the family.* Diane ushered her in and shut the front door.

"You want some coffee dear, a soda?" she asked as she headed to the kitchen. "All my kids come visit and eat all my food, you're no different," she winked.

"Soda please," she said as she followed her into the kitchen. Diane grabbed a soda from the refrigerator, handed it to Jelena and leaned on the countertop.

"What's on ya' mind dear?"

Jelena sighed heavily. "I need a divorce and my ex is not signing the divorce papers."

"You've served him already?"

"Yes," she said, popping the top on the soda can to avoid eye contact. "He has the papers, he just won't sign them. He keeps calling, and I've been so busy lately with the work and the security issue with Jordan. I just don't have the energy to argue with him about the damn divorce. I don't even know what Florida law is, can I just proceed without him? How long do I have to wait?"

Diane went into her back pocket and pulled her phone out. She searched through it, and then her face lit up. Once she was finished with it she put it back in her pocket. Jelena felt her phone vibrate.

"I just sent you the contact information for Jessica Romano, she's John's sister and a divorce lawyer. She will help you, introduce yourself as Jordan's mate."

Jelena cringed. "I'm sorry," she apologized. "That was rude."

"It's fine, dear, there is a lot to get used to."

"Thank you," she said quietly.

Diane clasped her hands together and looked around the

kitchen. "Let's talk about Sunday's dinner before we talk about my ignorant son."

Jelena laughed. "Jordan only told me about it a couple days ago, I remember the monthly party and there is no way I can come up with something that rivals yours on such short notice." Jelena looked kind of nervous as she gauged Diane's response. "So, I am just going to stick to my roots and the menu will be straight from Puerto Rico."

"I have no experience with cooking Spanish food, can I help?" Diane responded kindly.

"Yes! Angela is coming over tomorrow morning to get started. You are more than welcomed to come help us."

The women left the kitchen and spent the next hour or so talking about how to plan Sunday dinners sprawled out on the couches. Jelena felt her phone vibrate and pulled it out. It was a text from Jordan, asking her to come home. She sighed, and Diane frowned, sitting up.

"Everything okay?"

"Jordan just texted asking me to come home,"

Diane relaxed. "He's just getting off work."

Jelena's eyes got wide. How could she not have thought about him having a job? All this property and him being able to hide Giovanni's crimes.

"I guess being attacked is something that comes with wher-ever I am living," Jelena said. Diane's face fell. Jelena cursed herself for saying that aloud. "I'm sorry, that was rude."

"Just give him a chance honey," Diane said. "This is as new to him as it is to you."

"It's not like I can change my mind now."

Diane slid over and put her hand on Jelena's shoulder. "Ev-erything is going to work out."

Jelena rose from the couch. She hugged and thanked Diane for her hospitality.

"You're family dear, anytime."

#

Jelena pulled into Jordan's driveway. She spent the little drive thinking about the text. "Come home" he said. That means they were sharing a house. She did stay here all the time but with nothing more than a go bag. She stopped back by her house often to grab stuff and switch out clothes.

Getting out of the car she walked up to the front door and grabbed the handle. The knob didn't turn, instead a speaker by the door said 'Jelena Cohert welcome.' Then the door clicked, and she was able to turn the knob. Confused, she closed the door behind her, heard it click and the same voice said 'All locked'. *He put in a new security system.* she thought.

"Come upstairs," Jordan yelled.

Once she got into the bedroom, Jordan had just gotten out of the shower. He went over and kissed her. "Give me one minute," he said, walking back to the bathroom. "I like to wash the office off me when I come home."

Jelena went over to the bed and sat down taking her shoes off. "What do you do?"

"I work in engineering,"

"Are you being modest?"

Jordan chuckled and came out of the bathroom. "I am the CEO of ONAMOR, the tech company."

"What degrees do you hold?"

Jordan walked over the bed, still wearing his towel and grabbed Jelena's feet, putting them on his lap.

"I have a B.S in engineering. My M.S is in cyber security and my PhD is in Computer Science. What about you?"

Jelena was so impressed she almost missed the question. "My B.S in Psychology and my M.S is in social work. I am a licenced in social work. No time for my PhD because I joined the FBI."

"What would you get your PhD in?" he asked, rubbing her feet.

Jelena leaned back on her hands. "Well I don't know. I am on a different career path now then I was when I got my degrees. Then I worked with children caught in the system, now I hunt killers. I would have to really do some searching for what I would want."

"You know you're not 55, you're not about to retire. You have plenty of time if you want to advance or change careers. Why not go back to working with kids?"

"Because I love this. When I first joined the FBI, it was out of necessity. I had just gotten a divorce, I wasn't talking to my father or brother." She faded off.

"What happened to your Mother?"

Jelena sighed. "I have a mother and younger sister, Ana and Jade Dominguez. My mother left when Oliver and I were younger and took Ana with her. We haven't seen her since. Oliver is talking to them now though." Jelena's voice cracked with the betrayal..

Jordan put Jelena's feet back on the ground and grabbed her by the waist, pulling her close to him, so he was cuddling with her and whispering in her ear. "Why does Oliver have a different last name?" he asked.

"My name was María Jelena Dominguez. After my first marriage I changed it to Jelena M.D. Then I got remarried and became Jelena Cohert. Oliver is my mother's child from another relationship. His father is a fool, so Papí adopted him when he was still really little. My mother didn't want to change his name, she wanted it to be his choice."

Jordan was silent for a moment, so long Jelena almost moved from her spot.

"Jacob is the oldest brother, and he is the one who challenged our father a few years ago for his spot as Alpha," Jordan began, stroking her hand. "It was a brutal fight and John had won. He was going to kill him, to send a message. He could have been satisfied that he would remain Alpha until Jonathan wanted to challenge him, which was still a few years out. That wasn't enough, Jacob was on the ground and he was going in for the kill shot. I couldn't let him kill my brother because of his ego."

Jordan paused, and Jelena was afraid if she moved he wouldn't continue his story. Jordan continued with a low voice full of emotion.

"Before I knew what I was doing, I attacked. I knew that attacking the Alpha during the Blood moon ritual meant I was staking my claim to the pack. I didn't want to be Alpha, I wanted to save my brother. After I won and John was down, my mother proclaimed to everyone that I was the new Alpha, to the Romano and North American packs. I didn't want it. I was satisfied with John keeping it because Jacob was okay. But that's not the way things work. So now I have so many responsibilities for keeping this pack together as well as solving all these problems from packs all over the country."

Jelena swore he was crying. She wouldn't dare turn around though, she didn't want to ruin the moment. She felt so bad for him, she never really thought of how hard having this job would be for him.

"It is so much work that I am not cut out for. My brothers and Amara all have a spouse and families. I am the bachelor baby brother, I wasn't prepared for this. I can't do this."

She finally turned around and looked at him. "We can," she said as she rubbed her hand through his hair.

Jordan grabbed both sides of her face, touching his forehead with hers. "I have been dying to hear you say that."

"I'm scared, and I don't know what to expect. My life is screwed up with the only thing working right is my job. I don't know how but we will make it through all of it."

Jordan kissed her fiercely. Jelena pushed him on his back, so she could straddle him. She kissed him with just as much passion, and hunger as he gave her. Jordan grinned and with impossible speed she was lying on her back on the bed with Jordan hovering over her.

He was leaning down inch by inch staring at her with gold flickering though his eyes. That sparkle was all she needed to send her in overdrive. She reached up grabbing him by the shoulders.

"Mr. and Mrs. Romano, Diane Romano is at the front door." The speaker blared through the house. Jelena squealed and pushed Jordan off her, rolling to the floor.

Jordan started to chuckle. "Relax, it's the new security system. It should have done the same thing to you when you came in."

Jelena relaxed, remembering what happened when she touched the doorknob. "It spoke through the whole house?" she asked.

"No, it doesn't do that for me and you, but it does for everyone else."

"Okay," Jelena said, processing. "Okay, you go get some clothes on and I'll go answer the door for Diane."

Jelena hurried down the stairs and opened the front door. She gaveDiane a big grin and Diane hugged her.

"He got locks on the doors," she said. "See, I told you." She released her and clasped her hands together. "I've got the boys to bring some pots and such over. Jordan doesn't have anything to cook with."

Jelena stepped aside as the Romano boys carried boxes inside.

Jacob smiled and titled his head up slightly. "Smells like we're interrupting," he chuckled. Jordan came down the stairs and threw a pillow from nearby at his brother. Thank god they both are wolves because with that shifter strength because it would have done damage to a normal person.

I said NO

Jelena was running around the kitchen plating food, cleaning up messes, and rearranging dishes. The speaker spoke, "FBI Deputy Director is at the front door. The camera detects three other individuals as well. Shall I ask them to touch the doorknob?"

Jelena yelled, "No."

Angela started chuckling. "You complained of no security and your man installed a smart security system connected to the fingerprint database." She rose up from her spot and went to go get the door. "I want one," she yelled through the house.

Jelena was wrapped up in making sure everything was ready when Angela said, "Umm Jelena, you might want to come."

"I invited Papí and Oliver Ang, just let them in."

"Remember when the speaker said it's Mr. Domínguez, plus three people."

Angela smiled at Jelena's family. "Just give her a minute to catch on, she's been stressed today."

Just then Jelena came running to the front door coming to a halt when she saw who the plus three was. "How dare you," she growled.

"Jelena, you said it is a family dinner. This is your family, all of us," Oliver shrugged.

"Jelena, stop this and let us in the house," Mr. Dominguez said.

"All do respect Mr. Dominguez," Angela began. "She didn't even want to invite you. So give her a minute to process the two additional people she doesn't want here who she hasn't seen in 30 years."

Jordan came down the stairs "I heard we have guests" he stood behind Jelena, looking out at the people standing in the doorway.

"Yeah," Jelena said dryly. "You've met Oliver. This is our father -"

"Dominguez," he interrupted, sticking his hand out. "I am her Father. This is her mother Jade and younger sister Ana."

Jordan looked a little taken back. "Oh, uhh" and then looked at Jelena unsure of what to do next.

"It will be enough people here for you to leave me alone. Do not tell anyone you are my Mother, no use lying to anyone." Jelena turned around and stalked back to the kitchen without another word. Jade's face fell, looking sad and guilty. Jordan gestured towards the living room. "The boss says it's okay so come in, make yourself at home."

The Dominguez family came in and Angela went back to the kitchen with Jelena. Jelena made herself busy, and soon the house was full of hungry Romanos.

"All this food," Angela said. "I've never seen so many Arroz con gandules, and pernil in my life!"

"You would be surprised how much my boys eat," Diane exclaimed as she entered the kitchen. "I met your family Jelena, I am so happy they are here. It seems not everyone knows that we shift."

"I didn't know everyone was coming," Jelena said dryly. "But, it is time to eat."

Diane made a mental note to ask about that later. She whistled, and then people started pouring into the kitchen.

Jelena was actually having a good time that she had almost forgotten her mother and sister's presence. She had avoided them all night; She didn't have anything nice to say to either one of them. The night was progressing nicely, and she was happy her first Sunday dinner turned out so nice. One of the little Romanos ran up to her. "Luna Jelena, is this your phone? It smells like you and it keeps ringing."

Jelena smiled and said thank you. She took the phone and answered it. A raspy voice on the other end said, "Agent Jelena Cohert."

Jelena: Yes, who is this?

Caller: I have Giovanni and if you want him back, you'll go to that jail of yours and let Andre out.

Jordan was at her side listening to the call in an instant.

Jelena: He is in that jail with him. There is no way you have him.

Caller: Oh, you don't know his uncle bailed him out, told him to run. Too bad wolfbane takes 48 hours to cycle out of a wolf's system. He was left helpless.

Jordan grabbed the phone and growled, "You hurt my nephew and I will kill you."

The caller laughed. "You have 48 hours to release Andre" and hung up the phone.

Jelena grabbed her phone and dialed a number. She put the phone to her ear and said "Get everyone out, except Ang," to Jordan. Then the other line picked up.

"Hello, this is Senior Agent Cohert. I need a trace on the last number that called his phone. I also need video feed from the shifter jail, inside and outside from the past four days sent to my cloud for me to access remotely."

"Yes, ma'am."

"¿Que pasó?" Angela asked as everyone walked into the kitchen..

"Giovanni has been kidnapped. They just called me, they want Andre Franklin in exchange for Giovanni."

Amara sprang forward. "Do it, do it. Get my son back." She turned towards Jordan. "Do whatever you need to do to get my son back."

"Enough Amara," John said and turned towards Jelena. "What do you know?"

"I don't know anything. Like, how did he get out. The caller said his Uncle bailed him out. The problem is they give the prisoners wolfsbane to prevent them from shifting. That stuff lasts 48 hours in the system. He was helpless to defend him himself."

Angela spoke up, "So are there any long-lost Romano boys or are the three in this room Giovanni's only uncles?"

Amara growled at her brothers. "Which one of you got my son kidnapped?"

The room was silent for several seconds. Finally, Jacob said "I needed to do something. I couldn't let this intruder ruin Giovanni's life," he said looking at Jelena with red eyes.

Jordan pinned Jacob to the wall in an instant.. "If you ever disrespect her again, I will end you myself."

Jacob struggled in Jordan's grip. "I'm your brother, why are you taking her side?"

"I told you to stay out of it, I told you the police would handle it." Jordan was squeezing Jacob's neck so hard he was struggling to breathe. Diane touched Jordan's arm. It took him a couple seconds to recognize his mother's touch. When he did he let Jacob go. Jacob hit the ground hard.

"Get up" Diane snapped.

Jacob got up off the floor, wheezing. "Your Alpha gave you a direct order. You think we like to leave Giovanni to the police? Have him go through the system? The Alpha said he would, therefore he is. You had no right to disobey an order given to you."

"Mother, Giovanni is family. We shouldn't let her come into the picture and ruin our family."

Diane slapped Jacob, hard, across the face. He looked at his mother in shock. "Why are you taking her side?" he asked.

"There is no side you fool. She is the Luna of this pact."

"That boy has been touching girls way before Jelena came into the picture, you idiot and you know it," John said.

Diane jumped in. "Jordan decided Giovanni would be left to the system before he met Jelena. No where in this scenario does it give you the right to disobey a direct order from the Alpha. Whether it comes from Jelena or Jordan. You lost that opportunity when you lost your challenge."

Jacob jerked back in shock. Diane had never brought up this lost challenge to his father. Before he had the chance to respond, Amara was in his face, "You could never accept the fact that Jordan is our Alpha. He always gives you chances because he feels sorry for you and he loves his older brother. My son is kidnapped by God knows who and Jelena is an FBI agent who cannot simply switch prisoners, no matter how much I want her to. You put my son in danger. If he dies because you are to stupid to know it takes wolf'bane 48 hours to leave your system I will kill you myself."

Amara turned and faced Jelena. "How are we going to get my

son back?"

Jelena looked at her father and Oliver and then at Amara and shrugged her shoulders "How do you catch a wolf in the woods?"

"You get a wolf to hunt him," Amara and Jordan responded.

How do you catch a wolf in the woods?

Cohert's father took Ana and Jade home. As they were leaving, they hovered around the door. She assumed waiting to see if she would say something to them. She had nothing to say.

Instead, she focused on getting things together for this manhunt, or, wolf hunt as it was. This was the first time in her entire career of working with the SID that she had shifters to help her hunt a shifter. Her gear was in her trunk. Along with an extra set for Rodriguez. Jordan had taken one from the day she showed him what they had, that one went to Oliver.

Cohert was sitting at her computer looking over the security footage. Jordan crowded behind her shoulder looking as well as other family members asking what she saw and what happened.

"Okay," she began. "The camera shows Jacob and Giovanni walking out of the jail."

"Does it show how bruised his face was. Does it show how bad they beat him?" Jacob interrupted angrily.

"Fighting happens in every prison Jacob," Cohert said, annoyed. "The only difference here is everyone is on the same playing field because the guards makes it so no one can shift. A tiger has no advantage over a fox. Just two men fighting. Maybe instead of coddling Giovanni, he should have been taught how to handle himself when he didn't have another Romano there."

Realizing that was too harsh she looked over to Amara and shrugged apologetically. "Sorry," she muttered.

"No, you're right. No matter how much I don't want to hear it. I always thought we would be there to protect Giovanni from anything. I never thought to prepare him in case we weren't."

"What else does the video show?" John bellowed.

"Jacob and Giovanni talk at the car for a moment. Jacob shoves a bag in Giovanni's hand, and he gets in the car and drives off. Giovanni turns and starts in the opposite direction. It looks like he is headed towards the back of the prison, around the fence. Then we have a shadow step out, but not far enough out so that the camera catches any distinguishing features. I can't even tell if it's male or female. The shadow goes behind the building following Giovanni. That's all I have."

Amara kept muttering over and over, "I swear if we don't find my son alive."

"What's the move?" Rodriguez asked, talking over her muttering.

"We will all drive to the jail." Monroe began. He got up and started to put his gear on. Cohert and Rodriguez followed suit. "Once there, the wolves will shift and lead the hunt. I will ride on Amara's back. Rodriguez will ride on Michales, and Cohert will ride on Jordan's back. When we get there, we will turn on our coms which stops all of you from communicating telepathically. It's a precaution since everyone cannot be trusted."

Cohert looked at Jacob who was in the corner getting more upset by the minute. Cohert was about to say something but Jordan beat her to it.

"If you can't control yourself, you can stay here."

"No, he is staying here." John said.

Jacob threw his hands in the air. "You are not the Alpha of the pack anymore. You can't go around throwing out orders."

"We are in this mess because you didn't listen to the Alpha you fool. As your Father I order you to stay. That word carries just as much weight as Jordan's."

Monroe jumped back in. "Okay then, If we can trust Amara to stay in line then I won't take away your ability to communicate. There will be no way for us to communicate with you though. We all have our coms. Cohert will take Jordan's lead and relay what is happening to my team through the coms."

"Excuse me, dear," Diane said. "Why have you three using your last names?"

"I know Mother, it's weird. When they are in work mode," Jordan interjected using his fingers to make air quotes. "Everyone gets called by their last name,"

"It is a way to separate personal from professional since Oliver is my brother and Angela is my best friend. When we are on the job everyone gets called by their last name, just like every other agent. Having a personal connection does not exclude the fact we are colleagues," Cohert provided.

Nodding Diane asked, "Since all of us have the same last name, are you going to have to make up names for us?"

"No," Cohert said. "Jordan has told me you recognize and respond to your name being called when you shift. That could be useful to us. We don't want to start calling you something you won't understand."

Cohert then spoke to the whole room. "We will carry the bags that our gear comes in. Once at the prison, we will put their clothes in the bag and carry it with us."

Rodriguez clasped her hands together excitedly. "Your clothes really shred when you shift?"

Ignoring her friend Cohert continued, "When we locate Giovanni everyone will return to human form. There will be absolutely no shifting unless you see another animal. We all have silver bullets, we have to assume the kidnappers do too."

Jordan had explained they get shot with silver while in wolf form they had a pretty low chance of recovering. Initially, she thought it was a great idea to have a group of wolves rush in with them.

Monroe jumped back in. "Even though we are going about this unconventionally we have to remember this is an FBI extraction. Our paperwork will be a lot easier if we do not need to explain how wolves and God knows what else aided us in retaining the fugitive."

"He is not a fugitive, Jacob bailed him out. He is a victim," Amara said firmly.

Monroe looked as if we wanted to object but decided against it. "What I am saying is, Amara or anyone else. You cannot go playing hero. When it comes down to it, the three of us are in charge, got it?"

Once the three cars pulled up to the prison grounds Cohert, who was driving the first car with Jordan, Rodriguez and Monroe, led the cars around to the back of the building. When they arrived she showed her badge and told the officer at the gate that he should have been informed she was coming. The guy nodded and opened the gate. They followed Cohert to the rear of the parking lot and got out of the car. Once everyone had their gear, Cohert led them to another gate. The guard nodded his head in respect. "Good evening," he said and then let them through the gate. They walked through, leaving prison property.

Once they were a few hundred yards away from the fence,

Cohert gave the cue and the Romanos shifted. They decided just to bring another set of clothes so everyone did not have to strip naked before shifting out here.

"Holy shit," Rodriguez said as she stared at the black, brown and grey wolves.

Jordan came up to her, those gold eyes she recognized instantly staring at her and leaned his head down to the ground. She climbed up and looked towards Monroe and Rodriguez. "Climb up" she encouraged.

Rodriguez eagerly climbed up Michaels' back but Monroe seemed more hesitant. The wolf standing in front of him was huge. She had to be seven feet tall from her foot to the top of her back and she was the smallest wolf here.

"All set?" Monroe asked, and when he got an affirmative, they turned their coms on. Monroe nodded his head at Cohert giving her permission to take the lead. Patting Jordan twice on the back, giving him his cue that it was go time.

\#

"We ready?" he asked his family telepathically. Everyone nodded and began sniffing.

"It is stronger this way" John nodded about 50 yards from Jordan. Jordan could smell pretty good himself but he was no match for John. That was one thing he didn't fight his father on, his nose was never wrong.

"Okay then, lets go," Jordan replied and started in the direction his father indicated. Jordan took the lead. Michaels and Amara were flanking him, keeping a few paces back. Diane and John were on either side of their children making the top half of a diamond.

The pack trotted through the now wooded area. They had switched directions a couple of times and Cohert was sure they were communicating telepathically. Jordan would stop, hesitate, slightly then they would change their paths. She made sure to communicate Monroe and Rodriguez every time he hesitated, letting them know they were changing paths.

Rodriguez could not control her "Ay, mierda" and "Estoy montando un lobo" comments to herself.

Cohert heard a crack and Diane whimpered. She turned to see her fall over Diane had what looked like a bear claw trap wrapped around her food. Cohert jumped down immediately, stumbling because she underestimated how high up she was, to go help her. The wolves gathered around but Rodriguez and Monroe had their weapons drawn and their backs to Cohert checking their surroundings.

Jordan must have instructed the rest of his family to do the same because the remaining wolves surrounded Diane and Cohert, protecting them, like Rodriguez and Monroe.

Cohert bent down and looked at the trap. It looked like there were two levers on each side. When she pushed those down the trap opened and Diane yanked her foot back, then flapped her ears causing Cohert to smile. Positive that Diane was okay, she went over to her mate and grabbed his snout with both of her hands. She stared into his eyes wishing she could tell him to be careful.

Back on their wolves the group began again,everyone was extra vigilant for traps. They were walking now, deciding it was best to slow the speed down. Jordan was still leading the pack but instead of their diamond formation everyone was in a straight line behind him. John at the rear.

As they continued through the now dense forest Cohert spotted seven more bear traps that she pointed out as they were close to them. She told Monroe and Rodriguez to tell them to touch the ear which is closest to the trap.

They came across a slope and the wolves went down clumsily causing Cohert to sit straight up trying to keep her balance and stay on Jordan's back. Jordan stumbled and all of a sudden something wrapped around Cohert's neck, slinging her off Jordan. She landed on the ground with a thud.

Jordan shifted back in human immediately and rushed to her side.

"¿Qúe mierda?" Rodriguez yelled. She was moving to get off Michaels' back when Cohert held up her hand.

Jordan was looking at her with panic and fear in his eyes. "How bad is it?" he asked.

"The fall hurt more than whatever the hell is wrapped around my neck. Can you see what it is? Can I just pull it?"

Jordan tilted her head from one side or the other, wiping the blood that was dripping to get a better look. He extended his claws on one hand and sliced the wire off of her neck.

"You have retractable claws" Rodriguez squealed while trying to whisper at the same time. Jordan looked at her, then back to Cohert chuckling.

John came trotting over with a wire in his mouth, he dropped it in front of Cohert and Jordan. Cohert picked it up while Jordan put bandages she brought in her bag around her neck. John looked at Cohert and then looked at a tree nearby. He did it a couple times, and Cohert understood what he was trying to say.

"You can shift back," Cohert said.

"Please, because I am trying my best not to look at my sister's naked boyfriend but y'all are killing me," Oliver said with his head buried in Amara's fur.

"This was hanging from the trees, we have to be careful. This is the second booby trap we've found. We must be getting close.

They predicted that shifters would be coming to save him," Cohert said.

The hunt continues

They were all back on their wolves. This time they leaned forward while riding, to miss any more wires. All of a sudden the wolves leaned down. The agents took the hint and got off their backs. They began to shift back to human form.

"Oh, God" Monroe muttered and spun around, putting his back towards the now naked family.

Rodriguez started giggling.She looked at Cohert and gave her an okay symbol with her hands. Cohert rolled her eyes. Once everyone was dressed Cohert asked, "I figure we are close?"

"There are a lot of different smells coming from about 100 yards that way," Jordan said pointing.

"There are at least three full humans. I smell Giovanni and at least one other shifter," John added.

"John has one of the best noses in North America. He is being modest making it seem like he doesn't know for sure how many there are. If he says there are four, there are four," Diane said matter-of-factly.

Monroe began to formulate the plan. "Okay, so we should keep our pairs. Jordan and Cohert, Rodriguez and Michaels and Amara and I. We will be in charge of neutralizing any threat.

Diane and John, you will extract the fug- Giovanni and bring him out 200 yards back this direction. Stay with him until the rest of us come, no matter what you hear. We stay in human form no matter what." Monroe looked around at everyone making sure his point was made. "Are we ready?" he asked.

Everyone turned and looked at Cohert while she and Rodriguez said "Yes sir" to Monroe.

Cohert looked around and was caught off guard by everyone staring at her. "We take our orders from our Alpha" John said.

"We are in the field," Monroe responded. "She takes her orders from me."

"Very well," he replied. "We are ready."

Monroe motioned for the three pairs to spread apart with Diane and John coming behind them. They had about three yards in between each pair.

"Stay sharp," Cohert whispered. "Remember the booby traps."

The closer they got, a cabin started to come into view. The agents couldn't make out any details yet, just that it was there. The trees were still too dense.

"I'm going to blame myself for not being able to see in the trees and branches, not because I don't have supersonic eyesight," Rodriguez said.

Jordan chuckled. "We can't see anything yet either, it's too dense out here. All that I see is the outline of what I am assuming is a cabin in the woods."

"Nice" Cohert said, getting his movie reference.

"What we do know is that my father was right. There are three full humans, one shifter and Giovanni. I can't smell anyone else."

"I find it hard to believe they put traps in the woods, expecting shifters but only have one shifter bodyguard," Cohert said.

Jordan began to answer but Cohert held up her hand to silence him. "We are about to lose cover," she said.

They were coming to the end of the dense forest.It was flat and manicured the rest of the way to the house.

"Jordan and Cohert, take the south side of the house. Amara and I will take the northside. Michaels and Rodriguez, follow us on the Northside. You two will secure the house. Diane and John go in, get Giovanni, and come out," Monroe barked out. "Go," without giving anyone room to object.

Jordan and Cohert make a beeline for the back of the house. Cohert was in front with her weapon in her hand, ready, but lowered. Jordan behind her moving swiftly. They reached the back door and Cohert spoke into the coms "Ready to breach."

Jordan was about to kick the door but Cohert whispered, "Wait."

Jordan stopped and looked at her. "What? You said ready to breach."

"Yeah, but I have to wait for Monroe to say breach. When we are out in the field we go by rank, he outranks me, double time. He is in charge at work."

The fight begins

The fight begins

In the front of the house Monroe and Rodriguez stood on either side of the front door with their weapons drawn. Amara was standing behind Monroe, to avoid being seen through the window that was behind her. Michaels was standing behind Rodriguez and also had his weapon drawn.

Diane and John decided not to leave the cover of the forest until they had to enter the house. They didn't want to get caught up in the fight since their only task was getting Giovanni.

Monroe spoke into his com "Breach on 3,2,1" and both Jordan and Michaels kicked the doors in. The two shifters kicked with so much strength the doors shattered. Cohert and Monroe entered the house yelling, "FBI!"

There was yelling in the house, and gunshots began to fly. "They are firing, the bullets may be silver, be prepared," Monroe yelled while clearing the first room and headed towards the left.

He headed down the hall with Amara close behind him. He was about to turn a corner and stopped at the edge of the wall with his weapon close to his chest. Monroe dropped one hand

and did a countdown on his fingers and then turned the corner with his gun raised. Amara was right behind him but got pushed back because something hit Monroe hard in the face and he went down, his gun sliding across the floor.

Amara stopped in her tracks. She smelled a full human, so she backed up behind the cover of the wall and waited for him to come out.

A few seconds later a man walked around the same corner holding two guns. She assumed it was his, and Monroe's, and Amara punched him twice in the face hard. The man flew backwards but fired a wild shot out of both guns, getting Amara in the arm on his way down.

Amara roared at the pain. She bent down and picked Monroe's com out of his ear, putting it in hers. Her arm was slack, and she had to exert a lot of strength to lift it. She extended her claws and picked the bullet out of her arm. She looked at it and roared when she saw a silver bullet between her fingers. She threw it on the floor, her eyes beginning to water.

"Suck it the fuck up," she muttered. "No fucking crying, save your son."

The silver coursing through her veins weakened her. She took both guns from the man and bashed his face in. She heard his bones cracking and shattering and blood splattered everywhere.

"The bullets are silver. Monroe got knocked out. I am dragging him outside and coming back in," she said into the com.

"Is he breathing?" Cohert asked giving Amara her full attention.

"He didn't get shot, he got hit with something." Amara said while dragging Monroe to the porch. She had his collar with her good arm and had to stop and take a break every couple feet.

The silver was weakening everything that made her a shifter.

Something hit her in the back on when she made it outside, trying to drag Monroe's body and she fell. She landed on her hands and feet, both guns fell and slid out of reach. She jumped up and spun around. Her body hurt, due to the silver and the hole in her arm.

She roared which startled the women who had hit her in the back with a bat. The women shuffled back a few steps but recovered quickly and swung the bat again. Amara caught the bat with her injured arm. She was too weak to yank it away. Instead, she punched the women with all the strength she could muster in the stomach with her other hand. The woman flew back and hit the ground hard.

Amara watched in shock, as the woman began picking herself off the ground.. She was not at full power and her arm felt like it was falling off. Amara threw the bat and raised her fists ready to fight,her right arm lagging slightly.

The woman charged at her. She stopped, and roundhoused Amara in the face. She didn't expect the kick, and she hit the floor with a thud. Amara spit out a tooth and whimpered.

The woman kicked again, this time hitting Amara right in the face. She fell on her back, blood dripping from her mouth and nose.

The woman went to go kick Amara again, but she was expecting it this time. Amara grabbed her foot and twisted her ankle, breaking it.

The woman cried out and Amara swung her with the last bit of strength she had, letting out a roar that shattered the windows on the porch. Smacking the woman's head into the porch banister, she her out. Amara crawled to Monroe and dragged him over to where she was.

She couldn't shift even though shifting aided the healing process, causing her to heal faster. She needed to wait and let it run its course. Once she dragged Monroe over her legs, she collapsed backwards. They were in the corner of the porch, hopefully well hidden. "Two humans down" she said into the com and then passed out.

\#

As Jordan and Cohert entered the back door, they found themselves in the kitchen. That room was clear, and they turned left going deeper into the house. Cohert had her weapon raised when all of a sudden she didn't feel Jordan behind her. She turned around and he was gone. She then heard a roar, one that didn't sound like Jordan.

She ran back into the kitchen and saw a man, just as tall as Jordan with thick blonde hair. He had Jordan in a choke hold. Cohert raised her weapon and said "FBI, release him or I will shoot."

The man stopped choking Jordan to raise him up and hold him as a shield. As soon as the man's grip loosed up Jordan sucked in a breath while simultaneously grabbing the man's bicep and flipping him over his shoulder to the ground.

"He's a lion," Jordan growled.

The lion on the ground landed face up. He kicked his feet out and tripped Jordan. Jordan hit the floor, and the lion extended his claws and embedded them in Jordan's thighs. The lion got to his knees and dragged his claws down Jordan's legs.

Jordan lets out a roar, extending his own claws. He reached out and embedded them in the lion's arm. The lion roared and two shots rang out, and the lion slumped over.

Cohert hit him twice in the back with silver, shattering his spine and instantly killing him.

"Damn good shot," Jordan remarked.

"Hell yeah," Cohert said.

Jordan retracted his claws and growled as he removed the lion's claws from his legs. Cohert heard Amara say two humans down in the coms. She responded "One shifter down."

Cohert looked at Jordan, who was struggling to stand with his injury. "Amara and Monroe took out two humans."

Diane and John saw the fight on the porch and came rushing out of the forest. They entered the house, quickly passing their daughter and the women she was fighting. As they were searching the house John heard bumping and stopped to sniff the air. He smelled his son and followed the scent.

John heard a roar followed by another one. One was coming from this level, the other one seemed farther away.

"There's got to be a lower level, a basement," he said, leading Diane through the house.

Finally, finding the door they rushed downstairs and found Giovanni in a cage. Rodriguez getting choked by a man straddling her. Michaels was slumped in the corner.

Diane runs over to Michaels. "He's been shot," she said.

She extended her claws and dug the bullets out. The man saw John extending his claws. He released Rodriguez to fumble for his gun. Rodriguez began to cough and wheeze. By the time the man gets his guns, John slashes his claws across the face of the man, leaving deep gashes. The man slumps on top of Rodriguez. His blood is pouring all over her and she pushes him aside.

With the bullet finally out of Michaels, he begins groaning. "Oh, thank God," Diane exclaimed.

"It is silver," Rodriquez said, examining the cage. "I don't know how to pick locks. That guy said they don't have the key. They weren't planning on letting him out."

"Wouldn't it be funny,if I could just lift the cage up." As she said it she raised the cage off the ground. There was no bottom.

"What the hell," she said, when she lifted it off Giovanni.

"They didn't need a full cage," John said. "Giovanni couldn't touch it."

Rodriguez felt for a pulse. "He's alive," she said.

John rushed over and picked Giovanni up. Rodriguez and Diane helped Michaels up the stairs. They started towards the spot, 200 yards past the forest entrance like Monroe had said. Once they hit the porch, they spotted Jordan and Cohert leaned over in the corner.

"What's wrong?" Rodriguez asked.

Cohert turned around and sighed. "Damn it," she exclaimed. "Michaels is hurt too?"

"What do you mean too?" Diane asked.

"Amara is hit in the arm by silver, she is weak. Monroe is unconscious." Cohert said.

"I am not that weak," Amara chimed in.

"You better not be," Jordan said. "I need you to walk because I have to carry him." He explained pointing at Monroe.

"I am bruised, Michaels was shot by silver too," Rodriguez explained.

"Is the bullet still in him?" Jordan and Cohert asked at the same time.

"No," Diane answered.

They headed back through the woods towards the cars. Diane and Rodriguez carried Michaels. John carried Giovanni and Jordan carried Monroe and Amara stumbled along.

Fix me up Doc'

Fix me up Doc'

The three cars made their way back to the Romano property. There is a woman standing on Jordan's doorstep when they arrive.

"That's Dr. Roland," Jelena explained.. Once inside Dr. Roland inspects everyone and treats Oliver first.

"I have to go in order from worst off to best off. The unconscious full human is first," she said.

Dr. Roland spent a few minutes with Oliver checking vitals and asked John to go get equipment from her car. He returned with a huge bag and some IV poles. She laid Oliver out on the floor, flat on his back and hooked him up to an IV.

Next she moved to Jonathan and Amara. She gave them both Ivs with antibiotics.

Going over to Giovanni, Dr. Roland checked his vitals. She stuck a swab in his mouth, and then put it in a circular container. Once the swab hit the liquid inside, it turned purple.

"He had wolfsbane in his system. A lot of it. I can give him an IV with some antibiotics but I am not sure whether that will help. He might need a hospital. This color is very rich, which indicates a lot of the drug. I don't have the proper tests and equipment to tell how much. Therefore, I cannot accurately tell how much medicine to give him," she explained t.

"Please, Dr. Roland" Amara pleaded from her place on the couch she was instructed not to move from. "Fix my son."

Dr. Roland hooked Giovanni up to an IV. She laid him on the floor similar to Oliver. "If he is not conscious by tomorrow morning, he needs to go to a hospital," she said looking at Amara.

Jordan came in the house, dropped Oliver off and went outside. He shifted, his injuries would heal quicker in wolf form because he didn't have silver in his system. Dr. Roland checked on Cohert's and Rodriguez' neck wounds, which were minor.

"If you are conscious with an IV wait two hours then have someone remove the needle and dispose of the bag. If someone is unconscious and wakes up, remove the IV immediately. If someone unconscious with an IV doesn't wake up by morning, they need to go to a hospital immediately," Dr. Roland instructed. John helped her bring her equipment back to her car.

"Alight kids," Diane said. "We are headed back home. We will be by tomorrow to check on everyone."

"I will stay here and be on IV check," Amara said.

Rodriguez was on her way to the door waving and saying "Adios" to everyone. She stopped and looked at Jelena. "We've rid the streets of criminals."

Jelena winked and replied, "Until next time."

\#

Jelena said her thank yous and goodbyes and went upstairs. She was in desperate need of a shower. Once she entered her room, she was startled to see a wolf laying down in the middle of the floor. Jordan had come up here to heal instead of roaming outside.

When she entered, he lifted his head slightly. He was such a beautiful creature. Jelena took off her clothes and left them in a pile on the floor. Shower forgotten, she went over and snuggled next to Jordan. He lifted his paw so she should cuddle closer to him.

Engulfed in the safety and comfort of her mate, Jelena fell asleep instantly.

As the sounds of nature seeped through the windows the next morning and the sunlight peeked through, Jelena and Jordan, Romano pack Alpha and his mate lay naked on the floor, asleep.

About the Author

Hey hey, y'all! What's up?

I'm Ashley Johnson—but if you're a fan of young adult fantasy, you might know me as Sheyanne Warren. I write mystery, suspense, and stories that keep you on the edge of your seat. Originally from Syracuse, New York, I now call Charlotte, North Carolina, home.

I have a master's degree in forensic psychology (yes, I'm fascinated by the human mind!) and spend my days shaping young minds as a middle school teacher. But long before I stepped into a classroom, I was a book-loving kid who found magic in words. When I was three, my grandparents took the TV out of my room and replaced it with a bookshelf—best decision ever! From that moment on, stories became my escape, my passion, and ultimately, my calling.

Writing has always been second nature to me, but for the longest time, I didn't realize becoming an author was *actually* within reach. It felt like an unspoken dream—something I carried in my heart without fully acknowledging. But now? I'm here, doing the thing I love, and I write with purpose.

Representation matters. It's not just a phrase; it's a commitment. I want my readers—no matter who they are or where they come from—to see themselves in the pages of my books. Whether it's a fantasy world filled with adventure or a gripping mystery with unexpected twists, I write stories that reflect the diversity and richness of real life. Because everyone deserves to be the hero of their own story.

So, if you love books that blend heart-pounding suspense, intriguing mysteries, and unforgettable characters, you're in the right place. Let's embark on this literary journey together!

You can connect with me on:

- https://foreversevenpress.com
- http://facebook.com/A.Johnson.Author
- https://instagram.com/a.johnson.author

Subscribe to my newsletter:

- https://foreversevenpress.com/links

Also by Ashley Johnson

Serial Killer, Con Artists and Jelena
In the gritty underbelly of law enforcement, meet Agent Jelena Cohert, a tenacious Latina with a haunted past that fuels her relentless pursuit of justice. Rising from the ashes of a troubled history, Jelena's journey to the FBI is a testament to her indomitable spirit. She is not completely honest with her husband, but that is for his good. She has connections in high places but only uses them when she is pushed. Now, assigned to track down the most infamous con artist of her generation, Jelena finds herself entangled in a web of deception that leads her to the edge of her abilities. As she digs deeper, a chilling revelation emerges—she's unwittingly crossed paths with a cunning serial killer. Caught between the pursuit of justice and the consequences of her actions, Agent Cohert must navigate a treacherous landscape of lies, betrayal, and danger. Will she be able to outsmart the con artist and bring the elusive serial killer to justice, or will she be proven to not be the smartest in the room? In this gripping crime fiction, follow Jelena Cohert as she battles not only the criminals she pursues but also the demons within, racing against time in a relentless quest.

Maria Dominguez - Prequel | A Jelena Cohert Novella

What makes a woman change her name, her career, and cut off the ones who she loves the most?María Dominguez is a firefly Latina fresh out of college. The newest Social Worker her heart breaks for the twins who just got put on her caseload. Her father sets her up on a blind date and her relationship hits fast forward. She believes she has everything she wants until she realizes juggling a demanding spouse and a demanding job makes for one exhausted girl. When things spiral out of control, she reaches out to her father and brother for help. Unable to convince them, she takes things into her own hands. Defending yourself doesn't make you a victim, it makes you a fighter. That's what she tells herself until she suspects her husband did something she can't forgive. She is sick of her husband, she is sick of her father, she is sick of her brother and she needs to make it on her own.Death to María Dominguez dies and hail Jelena M.D.

Jordan Romano - prequel | A Jelena Cohert Novella

I am my brothers keeper. Jordan Romano a wolf shifter and the is the youngest of 4 siblings. His life is good. He owns his own technology company, He has a different women in his bed every night. Then his world is turned upside down. His brother challenges his father for the crown. His father's shady dealings puts Jordan right in the cross hairs of danger. His first love is back in his life and confusing the hell out of him. Jordan has lived his life how he wants to – relaxing and easy going. What will he do with his full plate? Will he have to save his brother again? Listen to his parents and let the attack on his life go? Will he become a one woman man, with the one who turned into a playboy to begin with?

Sister Assassins

Dive into the story of three foster sisters - Nia, Valentina, and Kuan-Yin - who have had a traumatic event that changed their lives forever. After witnessing a crime that the police failed to solve, the sisters decide to take matters into their own hands and become vigilantes to protect their community. The sisters are determined to fight against injustice and crime in their neighborhood, by any means necessary. They use their skills and talents and work in the shadows. Nia, the eldest sister, has her own private practice and clean-up crew on call. Valentina loves to be at the Recreation Center with her babies but knows her way around a needle. Kuan is a charismatic social worker whose culinary expertise are to die for. As they work together to avenge the loss of their Mama, the sisters face many challenges, dangerous criminals, personal demons, and fine-ass men. But with the support of each other and the community they protect, they remain determined. As they delve deeper into the underworld of their hometown, the sisters must also confront the personal traumas that led them to this path and the emotional toll that their mission takes on them. Can they keep this up?

www.ingramcontent.com/pod-product-compliance
Lightning Source LLC
Chambersburg PA
CBHW020038310726

48970CB00007B/2316